"Dr. Hyatt. This is Jodie De Vanti."

She needn't have identified herself. He could tell it was her by the frost in her voice, the way the phone receiver was growing cold in his hand.

"I have a horse with a gaping wound on its shoulder and chest," she said, "and it needs to be stitched. Now."

"Then you'd better call Dr. Stewart."

"Dr. Stewart is *also* out." And he could tell she suspected a conspiracy...with good reason. No vet wanted to go to the Barton spread after what had happened to him.

"You might try one of the Elko vets."

Sam was ready to put the phone down when Jodie blurted, "Don't you take some kind of Hippocratic oath? Don't you owe something to this animal?"

"Sorry, I can't afford another lawsuit."

Dear Reader,

I grew up in a rural area and my family had their fair share of veterinary emergencies. Quite possibly the most memorable was when my horse, Murphy, shattered his leg while crossing a log near the top of a mountain. That story had a happy ending thanks to two heroes—my dad, who held up the horse for almost two hours, and the vet who drove fifty plus miles to cast Murphy's leg in less than ideal conditions. I was riding Murphy less than a year later.

I've always admired rural vets, who tend to be underpaid and overworked, but still head out every day to do their jobs, sometimes risking life and limb when their patients are less than cooperative. The hero of *Once and for All,* Sam Hyatt, is just such a vet. He cares about people and he cares about animals, which is why he grudgingly agrees to treat an injured horse at the Zephyr Valley Ranch, despite the fact that the owner of the ranch once sued him for malpractice.

Jodie De Vanti is managing the ranch during her father's absence and calls Sam because he's the only available vet. She believes he's incompetent, but soon discovers her error. Sam's not only good at what he does, he's pretty darned attractive. Unfortunately Jodie has a secret that makes it impossible for her and Sam to ever be together.

I hope you enjoy reading *Once and for All.* Please visit my Web site at www.jeanniewatt.com or contact me at jeanniewrites@gmail.com. I'd love to hear from you.

Best wishes,

Jeannie Watt

Once and for All

Jeannie Watt

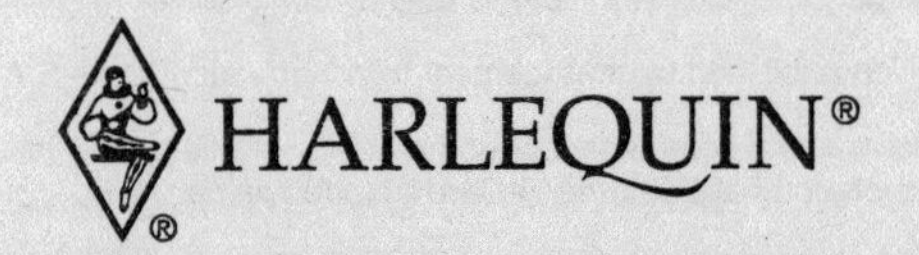

TORONTO • NEW YORK • LONDON
AMSTERDAM • PARIS • SYDNEY • HAMBURG
STOCKHOLM • ATHENS • TOKYO • MILAN • MADRID
PRAGUE • WARSAW • BUDAPEST • AUCKLAND

ISBN-13: 978-0-373-71647-0

ONCE AND FOR ALL

This edition published by arrangement with Harlequin Books S.A.

For questions and comments about the quality of this book please contact us at Customer_eCare@Harlequin.ca.

www.eHarlequin.com

Printed in U.S.A.

ABOUT THE AUTHOR

Jeannie Watt lives with her husband in the heart of Nevada ranch country. Since she owns no cows—only horses and ponies—she gets to experience calving season vicariously. When she's not writing, Jeannie enjoys reading, sewing and making mosaic mirrors.

Books by Jeannie Watt

HARLEQUIN SUPERROMANCE

1379—A DIFFICULT WOMAN
1444—THE HORSEMAN'S SECRET
1474—THE BROTHER RETURNS
1520—COP ON LOAN
1543—A COWBOY'S REDEMPTION
1576—COWBOY COMES BACK
1628—ALWAYS A TEMP

I want to thank my mom, who deals with calving every spring, for all the stories and information. Honest, Mom—if I lived closer, I'd take my turn checking the heavy cows at midnight and 2:00 a.m.

I'd also like to thank my friend Marcia Swift for once suggesting Beau and Ty as the perfect names for twins.

CHAPTER ONE

"SAM! It's the Barton ranch. Emergency."

Sam Hyatt looked up from his desk, where he was organizing the scattered papers into priority piles. He'd spent almost three minutes trying to catch up on at least five days worth of paperwork. "Tell them I'm not available." He couldn't believe Joe Barton had the balls to call.

Katie Murray nodded with satisfaction and walked back into her part of the vet clinic before saying in her professional tone, "I'm sorry. Dr. Hyatt isn't available."

Sam could hear the voice on the other end of the line from where he sat, and it wasn't the owner of the Zephyr Valley Ranch. The voice belonged to a woman.

"I'm sorry. He's not available." More squawking, then Katie said haughtily, "So why don't you sue us? Oh, yeah. I forgot. It didn't work out very well for you the last time, did it?"

Sam stood and crossed the office in a few long strides.

"Katie." His tech glanced back at him, her strawberry-blond ponytail swinging over her shoulder. She had good old Irish fight in her eyes. "I'll handle this." He took the phone. "Sam Hyatt."

"Dr. Hyatt. This is Jodie De Vanti." She needn't have identified herself. He could tell it was her by the frost in her voice, the way the phone receiver was growing cold in his hand. "I have a horse with a gaping wound on its shoulder and chest and it needs to be stitched. Now."

"Then you'd better call Dr. Stewart."

"Dr. Stewart is *also* out." He could tell she suspected a conspiracy…and with good reason. No vet wanted to go to the Barton spread after what had happened to Sam.

"Sorry. You might try one of the vets in Elko."

Sam was ready to put the phone down when Jodie blurted, "Don't you take some kind of Hippocratic oath? Don't you owe something to this animal?"

"I can't afford another lawsuit."

She was so silent that he wondered for a moment if the connection had been broken. Then she cleared her throat. "I guarantee, regardless of the outcome, no lawsuit."

"What if I have to put the horse down?" That was how he'd gotten into trouble the last time.

"You shouldn't have to." Sam said nothing. "But if you do, then there will be no repercussions."

Katie was staring at him, her lips pressed so tightly together that they were turning white. She slowly shook her head.

"My father isn't here," Jodie continued, her voice cool, but not icy like before. "Mike is gone, too. It's just me and Margarite. I need some help."

Sam turned his gaze to the ceiling. Not only did he feel for the horse, but three minutes at his desk had driven home the point that he could use the money. The Bartons always paid cash up front. They could afford to, unlike many of his other clients.

"How bad?"

"Bad, or I wouldn't be calling you."

No doubt. They'd tried to ruin him once. Ironic that because they'd failed, he was available to help now. "Give me forty minutes."

"Sam," Katie said as he hung up the phone. "No."

He didn't answer. Last time he'd checked, he was the boss of the outfit. He went back into the mudroom, shrugged into his canvas coat, stuck his feet into his insulated boots.

"Don't forget your Elmer Fudd hat," Katie said resignedly, holding out the plaid wool hat with the earflaps and fuzzy red ball on top. A gag Christmas gift to him from his nephews. Stupid-looking but warm when the north wind was blowing, as it was now.

"Thanks."

"Sam?" Katie said as he headed out the back door. He stopped, his hand on the knob. "Watch yourself."

He smiled. "You bet."

WAS HE EVER going to get there?

Jodie De Vanti stood at the horse's head, smoothing a hand over his nose, trying not to look at the pool of blood forming in the snow after running down the gelding's shoulder and leg. If Sam Hyatt didn't arrive soon, the horse was going to bleed to death. She just knew it.

"Are you all right?" Margarite called from the gate. The housekeeper hated snow and she hated blood, even more than Jodie did. For being ranch raised, the woman was surprisingly squeamish, and since someone had to be with the animal, Jodie had sucked it up and volunteered.

"I'm fine," she called back. Even though her voice shook—more from reaction than from cold—she couldn't keep the note of bitter irony out of it. Of course she wasn't all right. She was dealing with a bleeding horse and waiting for an incompetent vet.

But any vet was better than no vet, so she'd take what she could get.

The puddle of blood was getting larger, spreading darkly through the crystalline snow.

"Hold on, big boy," Jodie murmured, averting her eyes. The horse's knees started to buckle. He was going down, into the snow. "No..." She desperately hauled on the halter. All that did was to raise the animal's nose and keep it up as he collapsed. *Shit.*

"Don't you dare die," she muttered as she let the horse have its head. Her father would kill her, since it was quite possibly her fault the horse was all cut to pieces. And besides that...she didn't know if she could live with herself if she was responsible for this beautiful animal's death.

"Where *are* you, Sam Hyatt?" she yelled, scuffing her foot into the snow and kicking a small spray away from the horse.

"Are you all right?" Margarite called again.

"Fine."

Just then headlights appeared around a bend in the driveway, bobbing up and down as the truck went into the little dip before the last rise up to the ranch house. *Thank goodness.*

"Okay. It's going to be okay," she said to the horse. She'd never spent that much time around animals. Her mother was allergic to dogs and cats, so they'd never had family pets when she was a child. Then what did her father do? He moved her mother to a Nevada ranch after selling the investment firm he'd built from the ground up. Still no dogs and cats—in the house, anyway—but lots of cattle and horses. The crazy thing was, her mother had settled in without complaint. She seemed to enjoy country life.

Not Jodie. She appreciated the occasional holiday or long weekend, but right now—especially right now—she wanted to get back to Vegas. Back to the law firm where she worked, a place where she actually felt competent and could indulge in her need to overachieve.

The truck stopped next to the pump house and Sam got out. He opened one of the exterior panels and removed a kit. Margarite was already at his side, talking and waving. He nodded once and then gestured toward the house. Margarite didn't need a second invitation. She scuttled inside as Sam began walking toward the gate.

He was a big man. Not so much broad as tall and

sturdy. Fair-haired and gray eyed. Striking really, if one favored Vikings. Jodie favored sophistication and dark good looks—a preference that had gotten her into trouble in the past. Her restaurateur ex-husband had been dark and sophisticated. He was also no longer in her life, although his name remained. She'd started building her legal career as Jodie De Vanti and kept the surname to avoid confusion.

Sam grimaced as he shone the flashlight on the horse, took in the cuts on its chest, shoulder and legs. "What happened?"

"He got out of the pasture and one of the dogs spooked him. It was dark and he hit a piece of farm equipment. The disk."

Sam blew out a breath, then knelt down and started checking the horse's vital signs. "I'll need you to hold the light. We'll stitch him right here. I'm going to have to suture the muscle first on this bigger gash...."

Jodie swallowed and took the light. It shook. He shot her an impatient glance, which made her backbone stiffen.

"You can drop the lead rope. He's not going anywhere."

"Right." She did so and held the light with both hands. Sam went to the truck, then came jogging back with more equipment. A few minutes later the wounded area was numbed and he was stitching a gash. Or Jodie assumed he was. She couldn't make herself watch.

"Hold the damned light steady."

"I'm trying."

"It would help if you watched where you were shining it."

"I don't see how my fainting would help anything," she said, though she ventured a glance.

His hands stilled momentarily before he pulled the thread on through the flesh, did a few fancy passes with the suturing needle, then snipped the thread.

"Blood makes you faint?"

"I'm not a fan." It was the needle going into the skin that made her queasy at the moment.

"Great," he muttered.

"You could have brought an assistant."

"So you could sue the pair of us?"

"That's uncalled for."

Sam didn't reply. He started stitching in a new area. The horse's chest was in ribbons and this was going to take a long, long time. Jodie bit her lip and fixed her eyes on the rise and fall of the gelding's ribcage.

BY THE TIME SAM HAD finished sewing up the horse, his fingers were numb and his legs were cramped from being in almost the same position the entire time. But thanks to the cold, the blood had flowed slowly, so the animal hadn't lost a significant amount, and Sam was able to get the poor horse put back together. He sat back on his heels, surveying his work. What a damned shame. This gelding was a beautiful animal, and now he would be scarred for life. Joe Barton, Jodie's father, wouldn't be able to ride him to impress people, and he was gelded so he couldn't breed him. Sam wondered just what he would do with him. The horse would probably make a decent pleasure ride.

Sam glanced at Jodie, who was staring sightlessly at

the rows of neat black sutures crisscrossing the horse's chest and foreleg. She'd lost her cool, all-business demeanor. In fact, she appeared to be done in. Her dark blond hair, longer in the front than in the back, was jammed behind her ears, her face was pale and there were smudges of mascara under her eyes.

"How'd he get loose?" The shift in Jodie's expression was brief, fleeting, but he caught it. "Did you forget to latch the gate?" he asked as he got to his feet. She didn't answer. The reveal-nothing lawyer expression was once again in place, and he had to admit she carried it off well, even with mascara where it didn't belong.

The horse was starting to make an effort to get back to his feet, and Sam assisted him all he could, pulling up on the lead rope to help the gelding keep his balance. Finally the animal heaved himself up, and all the stitches held. The first hurdle had been cleared.

"Is there a place in the barn for him?"

Stupid question. Most people didn't have homes as nice as Joe Barton's new barn. And Sam bet that this horse had his own stall with a brass nameplate.

"Will I need to give him any medication?" Jodie asked after they had slowly walked the horse to the barn and then released him into a large box stall used for foaling.

"Yeah. I'll get that. And I have some written instructions for you to follow." It was snowing lightly when they left the barn and headed to the truck. Sam was glad Mother Nature had held off for a while. Usually when she had a January blizzard in store, she made certain he was doing something critical in the middle of it.

Once they reached his vehicle, he opened a frosted utility panel and pulled out a bottle of penicillin. "He'll need 20 cc's twice a day the first couple days."

"With a needle?" Jodie took a step backward, her hand rising to her chest.

"With a needle," he agreed, holding the bottle out. She accepted it gingerly.

"Will you come back to give the shots?" Sam gave a small negative shake of his head and Jodie's eyes went a little wild. "I can't…."

"I'll leave the syringes, too."

"No," she stated adamantly.

Under other circumstances it would have been amusing to see the calm, collected lawyer knocked out of her comfort zone by something as simple as an injection. But these were not ordinary circumstances and there was nothing amusing about the Bartons.

"When's your father getting back?" He knew from the very efficient grapevine that Joe Barton had left the day after Christmas for a long vacation in Europe.

"Weeks from now."

"How about your worthless foreman?"

Jodie didn't even blink at the insult, which Sam felt totally justified in delivering. The arrogant SOB had tried to testify against him in the malpractice suit. He'd come off looking stupid—one of the few satisfactions Sam had had during the trial, with the exception of the not guilty verdict.

"Chandler quit just after Thanksgiving," she said stiffly.

Thank goodness, Sam thought, wondering if perhaps

Joe had finally fired him. When the foreman had testified at Sam's trial, he'd smugly announced he had degrees in human resources and agribusiness, but hadn't said a word about being a ranching menace.

"What about the other hand?" Joe had hired a cowboy with some veterinary training when he'd come to realize that no vet in the area would service his ranch. For the big jobs he flew in a fancy vet from Las Vegas.

"Mike is in Idaho visiting family." Her expression grew more hopeful. "But he'll be back in two days. You'd have to make only a couple trips…."

Sam hated people who wouldn't take no for an answer. "Lady, I'm not driving thirty miles to give an injection. Besides—"

"You know I'll pay you," she interrupted. "I'll pay you right now if you want."

"I have other clients that need my services."

"But like I said," Jodie replied significantly, "I'll *pay* you."

"Times are rough," Sam snapped. He wasn't going to have this rich bitch looking down her nose at his friends and neighbors who sometimes couldn't make payments. "And I was about to tell you that Margarite can give a shot if she has to."

"Really?" Jodie seemed shocked at the idea, though why, he didn't know. Injections were common on a ranch and Margarite had grown up on a huge one up north.

"Yes." Sam pushed back the edge of his coat sleeve and glanced at his watch. He might just make it back for the second half of his nephews' basketball game. "I want to be paid now."

"Don't trust me?" Jodie asked sardonically.

"Don't want to see you again."

She stilled, but her expression didn't change. "That's to the point."

Sam shrugged. "It'll take me a few minutes to calculate the bill."

"Calculate away." She strode off toward the house, which was about twice the size it used to be now that Joe Barton was done pouring a boatload of money into it.

Sam charged full price and then some for the after-hours call. By the time Jodie came back with a checkbook he had the figures for her.

"What's the damage?"

He held out the paper, which she slowly scanned, noting each item. Then she began to write. What would it feel like, Sam wondered, to write a check for that amount and not tell the recipient to please hold it for a day or two while he transferred funds to cover it?

"Thank you for coming," she said briskly. Then her eyes traveled upward to the top of his head. To the Elmer Fudd hat.

Sam's mouth tightened as he took the check, written on the ranch account. He hoped hers was one of the authorized signatures, since Tim Paulsen at the bank would notice. Jodie didn't actually live at the ranch, but visited when the whim hit her. The rest of the time she spent in Las Vegas, practicing law.

"Thanks." He folded the check once and shoved it

into his pocket before walking back to the truck. Mission accomplished. Now he hoped he never had to set foot on the Barton ranch again.

JODIE CHECKED THE HORSE at ten o'clock and then again at midnight, tromping through the snow to the barn in silk pajamas, a down coat and insulated rubber boots. Usually Mike, her father's cowboy, had trails cleared between the buildings, but it had snowed during his days off and Jodie hadn't yet gotten around to shoveling the paths. Snow was not something she dealt with in Las Vegas, but after growing up in Chicago, she'd had enough white stuff to last her a lifetime.

Bronson was lying down when Jodie came in through the side door, as he'd been the last time she'd checked. But now he lifted his head and seemed more alert as she approached the stall. She couldn't believe the number of sutures Sam had so patiently tied in the cold and dark, while the light she was supposed to be holding steady wavered about. Maybe he had made a fatal mistake with her father's horse last year, but he'd done a good job tonight. The horse would have bled to death if he hadn't relented and agreed to treat the animal.

Was it her fault that the horse had gotten out in the first place? She honestly didn't know. The gate had been open when she'd found him, injured and bleeding, and she had used it earlier that day. Margarite had gone through it, too. One of them was responsible.

Even if it wasn't her fault, Jodie felt like crap. She hated making mistakes. She pushed her hands into the pockets of the down coat and watched as the horse tucked his nose to his chest and closed his eyes. A few minutes later she left the barn. She needed to get some sleep.

Or try to.

Margarite was in the kitchen tidying up when Jodie walked into the covered porch. The woman's charcoal-colored hair was rolled into pin curls—something Jodie hadn't seen since her grandmother had passed away—and she was wearing a blue fuzzy robe that zipped from her ankles to her chin. Quite the look, but somehow Margarite managed to pull it off with an air of dignity.

"Do you want some tea or something?" she asked through the open door to the porch as Jodie slipped out of her boots and hung up the coat she'd worn over her pajamas.

"No. Thanks." She padded into the kitchen in her stocking feet, ruffling her hair to shake off the droplets of water from melting snowflakes.

"Is he okay?" Margarite folded the dishcloth she'd been using to wipe down the counters, then adjusted the stools at the breakfast bar. The housekeeper liked everything to be just so. Margarite would have latched the gate all the way.

"So far." Jodie hoped he stayed okay or she'd have even more explaining to do to her father.

"He'll recover." The housekeeper snapped off the kitchen light and both women walked through the dining room to the staircase.

Again Jodie felt a wave of guilt.

Margarite tilted her chin up to look Jodie straight in the eye. "Accidents happen on ranches." Her voice was stern. "Understand?"

"Yeah." Jodie pressed her lips together. "Are you sure you can give the shot tomorrow?"

Margarite's face contorted into an expression of prolonged suffering. "Yes, I can give the shot if you can hold the horse. But the *very instant* Mike gets back, he's taking over. I hate to give penicillin. It's a very thick liquid and the needle's big and it takes forever—"

Jodie held up a hand. "Thanks. I understand." She gave a shudder and headed for her bedroom. So much for sleeping.

CHAPTER TWO

"WHY AREN'T YOU at practice?" Sam frowned as Beau, one of his twin nephews, came in through the front door of the vet clinic, the bells Katie had attached to the door announcing his entrance.

"I'm ineligible this week."

"What?" Sam stood up behind the desk. At fifteen, Beau was almost as tall as him, but was still very much a kid inside—a kid who wasn't doing too well in school. "I thought you said you had your classes under control."

Beau flashed him an angry look. "I thought I did have them under control."

"Which one?"

"Guess."

Sam didn't need to. Math. As always. Beau's twin, Tyler, didn't have as much trouble with the subject as Beau did, but Ty couldn't seem to explain the concepts to his brother. Heaven knew he'd tried, since Beau was six feet two inches tall and the top scorer on the basketball team. Ty was a quarter inch shorter and two points behind Beau in the stats. The team did all right with one brother, but with two, they were a force to be reckoned with.

"How bad?"

Beau swallowed as he glanced down, blond hair falling over his forehead. "A little lower than a D."

"How much lower?"

"Fifty-five percent." Beau dropped his backpack, which must have weighed forty pounds, judging from the sound it made when it hit the floor. "It was that last test." He all but exploded as he said it. "I don't get it. I studied the chapter and I thought I understood *everything.*"

Sam swallowed his anger. Beau was clearly upset, and the boy had spent way too much time close to tears over the past year and a half. "How'd Ty do?" he asked quietly.

"He passed. Of course."

Sam moved out from behind the desk and crossed the room. He put a hand on the kid's shoulder, then pulled him into a rough embrace. He didn't know what else to do. How could he tell if Beau was honestly doing all he could to pass his classes, or whether he was putting in a moderate effort and hoping for the best? Sam had been in this parenting gig for only eighteen months, since his brother and sister-in-law were killed by a drunken driver while crossing a street in Las Vegas, and he'd received custody of their sons.

He let out a breath. He'd forgotten what hell the teen years could be, but he was reexperiencing them now in living color.

"What am I going to do?" Beau muttered before stepping back. He tipped his chin up, stared at the ceiling.

"You're going to get your ass in a chair and work on

math tonight. We have a couple days to raise your grade before the next eligibility check. Have you talked to the teacher?"

"No."

"E-mail her. See what she has to say, what you need to work on. Then after supper we're going over that test."

As it turned out, though, Sam didn't have the time. He and Beau had just settled at the kitchen table with pad, pencil and failed test paper in front of them when the phone rang.

"It's the Taylor ranch," Tyler called from Sam's den.

Sam reached for the extension. One of the Taylors' show mares had kicked its leg through a fencing panel and got hung up. The leg was swollen almost double and the owners suspected she might have a broken tibia.

He climbed into his canvas bib overalls, clamped the plaid wool hat on his head. "Listen," he said in a low voice to Tyler. "Get your test and sit down with your brother and see what the two of you can figure out."

"But—"

Sam had been a parent long enough to perfect The Look, which he now employed full force. "You want your brother eligible, right?"

"Right."

"Then I don't care if you have other plans. Help him out."

"All right."

"HAVE YOU HEARD FROM MIKE?" Jodie asked as Margarite pulled a casserole out of the oven. The housekeeper's lasagna was made with cottage cheese and ground beef—not really lasagna, in Jodie's opinion, but surprisingly tasty.

"No." Margarite set the dish on a cast-iron trivet, then closed the oven door.

"I'm worried." Jodie paced to the picture window behind the dining room table and peered outside, hoping to see headlights. Mike had been due back from Idaho the day before. There'd been a storm to the north, so Jodie had assumed he'd waited to travel, and simply hadn't bothered to call. But now he was more than twenty-four hours overdue and she hadn't heard a word.

"You're worried?" Margarite muttered from behind her. "I'm the one manning the syringe." She'd already tried to coax Jodie into giving an injection, but Jodie couldn't do it. Her fear of blood and needles was even greater than Margarite's. What a team they made.

"I guess I'll go through his file, see if his cell number's there."

"Eat first. Mike will probably be here by the time you're finished." Margarite set a salad on the counter next to the casserole, then held a plate out to Jodie. "He'd better be here."

Jodie had tried to convince her that official cooking wasn't necessary while her parents were gone, but Margarite was having none of that. She was paid to cook and she was going to put meals on the table—or the counter, as she'd done tonight, since they were eating buffet style.

After dinner there was still no sign of Mike, so Jodie

went into her father's office and opened the top drawer of the big oak file cabinet where Joe Barton kept paperwork for every employee that had come and gone since he'd bought his ranch three years ago. And there had been quite a steady stream of comings and goings. Jodie's father was not an easy man to work for. He demanded a level of expertise and commitment that many people simply didn't have anymore. Even Chandler had unexpectedly quit, which had in turn set off a major family argument.

Her father had immediately tried to cancel the European vacation her mother had been planning for almost a year. Jodie's normally complacent mom had leveled threats, since she firmly believed her husband's heart problems, which he refused to take seriously, stemmed from managing the ranch. Jodie had eventually come to the rescue, grudgingly taking a sabbatical so that she could look after the property during the eight weeks her parents would be touring southern Europe. It was the only way her father would agree to leave, and even then it had been an uphill battle convincing him to go.

"Damn it, I know it's here," Jodie muttered as she flipped through the manila folders, beating up her cuticles in the process. Her dad kept a hard copy of everything. She dug deep and finally found Mike's file toward the back of the drawer and pulled it out. His cell number was there, so she dialed it from the office phone. No answer. Jodie jotted down the number and put the file away, telling herself not to worry. He was probably on the road, stranded somewhere with no service. It happened.

And it also meant that she and Margarite were about to embark on another adventure into veterinary care.

"Anything?" Margarite asked hopefully when Jodie returned to the kitchen.

She shook her head.

"I was afraid of that." The housekeeper went into the mudroom, stoically put her feet, shoes and all, into rubber galoshes, and pulled a coat off the hook. Next came the giant black scarf, wrapped twice around her neck and knotted, the wool hat and finally gloves. Jodie had watched the procedure enough times during the past few days to know all the moves.

"Ready?" the older woman asked.

Jodie had already slipped her feet into boots and put on a coat. She could make it to the heated barn and back to the house without a hat or gloves.

Bronson limped painfully to the back of his stall when he saw them coming. He'd figured out that when Margarite showed up, a painful jab was soon to follow. Horses were a lot smarter than Jodie had first assumed.

She went into the stall and slipped the halter on the big horse, who gave her an equine look of sad resignation. Margarite's expression wasn't that much different as she entered the stall. She held up the penicillin bottle, stabbed the needle through the rubber opening and measured out the dosage. Then, needle in hand, she pounded her small fist on the horse's hip a couple times to deaden the area, before she masterfully slipped just the needle into the muscle and attached the loaded syringe. Bronson bobbed his head up and down, but stood still as Margarite slowly pushed the plunger until it stopped, then removed the needle. As always, her face was pale when she finished.

"I hope Mike is here bright and early tomorrow morning," she grumbled as they made their way along the snowy path to the house.

"He may even arrive tonight," Jodie said, but she was getting a bad feeling about this. Mike should have called by now.

She tried to reach him two more times that evening from the ranch phone, and then, wondering if he recognized the ranch number and wasn't answering on purpose, she dialed the number from her cell. A masculine voice said hello on the second ring.

"Is this Mike Bower?"

"Yes."

"This is Jodie De Vanti. When are you coming back to the ranch?"

There was a healthy silence before Mike said, "I'm not coming back."

Jodie's temples started to throb. *What the hell?* "Why not?"

"I found another job up here, closer to my family."

The throbbing intensified. "You do know that it's common courtesy to give notice of resignation?" She spoke the last words through her teeth.

"I was going to call tomorrow after everything was firmed up here," he confessed.

"And in the meantime, we're left hanging, you coward."

"Maybe if your dad wasn't such a jerk, I'd still be

there," Mike said, and he had the gall to sound justified. "But he is and I ain't." He hung up the phone, and it was all Jodie could do not to throw hers across the room.

What an asshole, blaming her father, and not being man enough to quit properly.

Jodie weighed her phone in her hand for a moment, then carefully set it on the desk.

Okay. She could handle this. She was used to thinking on her feet. The only problem was she did it in a courtroom or while working with a difficult client. This was different.

"He's not coming back," Jodie told Margarite when she came in with a cup of tea.

The housekeeper stopped in her tracks and the cup clattered on the saucer.

"Hey," Jodie said, trying to be as positive as possible, "is there any reason we can't handle the ranch on our own until Dad returns? It's only six and a half more weeks and so far so good…barring the horse incident." She wasn't wild about feeding in the subzero morning temps, but she'd do whatever she had to.

"Early calving."

"What?" Jodie asked, her eyes getting round.

"The early calves. Sometimes the cows have trouble. And if there's a blizzard, you can bet there's a cow out there having a calf in it. Mike was out at all hours last year."

Jodie went to the sideboard and poured two glasses of Malbec without bothering to ask Margarite if she wanted one. At this point they both needed a drink, and tea wasn't going to cut it.

"I am *so* pissed at Mike," Jodie muttered as she recorked the bottle with the crystal stopper. "At least he could have given some warning, the sniveling coward."

"I'm surprised he didn't leave sooner," Margarite said matter-of-factly, accepting the glass after setting the porcelain teacup on the end table next to the leather sofa.

"Why?" Jodie asked. She had her own opinion—Mike was spineless—but was curious to hear the housekeeper's take on the matter.

"Frankly, when things go wrong, your dad tends to fire from the hip. Mike and Chandler took a lot of heat over the past year."

"Were they responsible for what went wrong?" Jodie asked reasonably, knowing that while her father was a tough man to work for, he set the same standards for himself that he set for others. She had spent her life living up to those standards and it had made her a stronger, more capable person.

"Not always," Margarite said. "Sometimes Mother Nature was responsible. Your father came down on Mike pretty hard a time or two for things that were out of his control." She shrugged her thin shoulders. "And Mike doesn't take criticism well. I think the only reason he stayed as long as he did was because there were no other job opportunities."

"Well, apparently one just arose," Jodie said darkly, taking a healthy swallow of wine, "and now I have to try to hire a cowboy before this early calving starts."

She stared into her glass, slowly swirling the contents. Where did one start? The employment office? *Hi. Do you have any cowboys?*

"Yeah, you need to do that." Margarite hesitated in a way that made Jodie glance up. "But without Mike... you're also going to have to find a vet that'll come out here. Sometimes they have to C-section the cows."

Jodie stopped swirling. "You're kidding." A vet. Willing to come out here. She'd practically had to promise her firstborn to get Sam to the ranch, and despite the decent job he had done on the stitches, she still didn't have a lot of faith in his vet skills. Maybe sutures were his forte. Since her father had buried a thirty-thousand-dollar horse, internal medicine obviously was not.

"I'm not kidding one bit. Your dad bred the heifers to a big bull to get black calves."

Jodie blinked at the housekeeper. "Why did he need black calves?"

"Black cattle sell for a few cents more a pound."

Jodie couldn't even begin to find the logic in that. It wasn't as if the person consuming the cow knew what color it had been. She slumped back against the sofa cushions, reminding herself that this, too, would pass.

"Lucas is back in town."

Jodie stared at Margarite over her glass.

"Wasn't he in rehab?"

"Yes."

"Didn't my dad fire him for drinking on the job?"

"Yes."

Jodie closed her eyes. Debated. What the heck? "Do you know how to get hold of him?"

"I can find him. I know his sister."

"Think he'd work temporarily?"

"We can ask."

"Let's do that."

Margarite made a few calls, tracked Lucas down, and then Jodie phoned him. The cowboy was more than happy to put in a few weeks at the ranch while Joe was gone—with the understanding that if something permanent came up, he'd have to take it. He was in the middle of a job search.

Jodie agreed and hung up. Lucas might not be a vet, but he was a warm body and knew how to feed cattle and birth calves. Joe probably wouldn't approve of Lucas any more than Sam, but Joe wasn't going to know about any of this until he came back.

CHAPTER THREE

"YOU'RE NOT GOING TO believe this," Katie said as Sam came in from an early morning emergency call—a bull with a broken leg—that had segued into routine equine dental work in which the horse had not been all that eager to participate. He was tired and ready to believe anything. And he groaned when he saw what she was holding between her thumb and forefinger, as if it were a dead mouse.

"Whose check bounced?" He shrugged out of his canvas coat and hung it on a wooden peg. It was the third returned check that week. At this rate, he wasn't going to be able to pay his own bills. Given the choice, Sam would rather wrestle a prolapsed uterus back into a struggling cow than deal with billing and accounts receivable—although, since it was just after the holidays, his mailbox wasn't exactly spilling over with envelopes containing checks. And obviously, those that did arrive were not a guarantee of money in the bank.

"Mrs. Newland."

"Oh, man."

Mrs. Newland was a sweet lady devoted to her two

wild terriers. Sam didn't do a lot of small animal work, but when one of the dogs had been attacked by a coyote, he'd stitched it up after hours.

"I know. What do you want to do?"

"Call the bank before you redeposit. If there aren't enough funds to cover it, then bill her again."

Sam couldn't afford to do work gratis, much as he'd like to.

The bell on the back door rang, and Beau and Tyler, who were supposed to be on their way to school by now, came through the mudroom into the clinic office with a blast of cold air.

"We can't get the Beast started," Tyler said, rubbing his gloved hands together.

"For real?" The last time the boys had trouble starting the Beast was when Ty had a date and thought Sam's Ford crew cab would be more impressive than a tiny '94 Mazda pickup with a dented tailgate. Ty loved to impress. Beau was happy to just be himself.

"Yeah. I think it's the battery. We'll need a jump."

Sam plopped the Elmer Fudd hat back on his head and grabbed his gloves. Five minutes later the Beast was running and he was coiling his jumper cables.

"Good luck with that test," Sam said to Beau as the kid climbed behind the wheel. "You, too, Ty."

"You don't need luck when you're good," Tyler said with a confident smirk.

"You have a C."

"Whatever."

Sam opened his wallet and pulled out four twenties, which he passed to Ty through the open window. "Buy a battery for the Beast on the way home."

"Are you sure?" The boys were supposed to handle maintenance on the small truck.

"Yeah. I don't want you getting stranded somewhere." The teens could change the oil themselves. A battery seemed more of a parental responsibility. Sam may have had parenthood thrust upon him, but he was determined to do the very best he could.

IT HAD BEEN A WHILE SINCE Jodie had seen a more wonderful sight than Lucas Reynolds driving the tractor with the hay trailer behind it out into the field to feed the horses and cattle. Not that she and Margarite hadn't done a fine job of feeding, but enough was enough. She liked being inside with a cup of coffee rather than outside on the back of the trailer, freezing her ass off.

Margarite had been in a good mood since he'd showed up yesterday, the morning after Jodie called. No more injections, no more cold trips out to the haystack. Lucas Reynolds was indeed a knight in shining armor. Or rather a knight in a beat-up canvas coat, a ratty silk scarf and a battered felt cowboy hat. But the expression on his craggy face was relaxed and his eyes clear, quite a change since the last time Jodie had seen him, during a summer visit just before Joe fired him.

Margarite came into the dining room and set a list on the table beside Jodie's coffee cup. "I thought of a few more things I need in Elko, if you don't mind."

"Trust me. I don't mind." She was looking forward

to getting out of the house for a few hours, and had volunteered to go on a grocery run to town. While she was there, she'd stock up on books, see about a manicure, get the Spitfire serviced.

She called her law office as she drove north, and talked briefly to Penelope, the receptionist, who told Jodie that since she was on sabbatical, she needed to focus on things other than work. Besides, there was no gossip and no new cases of note. Things were running smoothly, but yes, they would run more smoothly once Jodie got back. And then Penelope had hung up on her.

Okay. Jodie dropped the phone onto the passenger seat. Point taken. No obsessing over work. She was on leave. She was supposed to relax and come back refreshed. No telling if that would actually happen, since she hadn't wanted to leave in the first place.

She reached for the phone again and called Gavin, the associate who had taken her unfinished cases. She enjoyed a few minutes of conversation and discovered the status of each case before he had to go. Jodie hated being away from the office, hated waking up in the morning with nothing to work on, no strategy to plan. But…at least her sabbatical had gotten Joe onto the airplane. The smile on her mom's face as she'd followed him into the security area had been worth the long empty hours Jodie was spending on the ranch.

When she arrived back in the late afternoon, the trunk of her small car loaded with groceries not available in Wesley's much smaller stores, she knew something was wrong. Lucas and Margarite were in the kitchen, talking in low voices, when she came in through the mudroom. The top of the housekeeper's head barely hit the tall cowboy's shoulder, but there was no doubt as to who was controlling the conversation. They turned in unison as she closed the door, and Jodie instantly knew she wasn't going to like what she was about to hear.

"I think we're going to need a vet," Lucas said before the door latched.

Jodie stared at the couple in disbelief. "Oh, just shoot me now."

"It's that new bull your dad bought before he left," Margarite said, her expression grim, as well it should be. Joe had spent a ton of money on that black bull because it was homozygous, whatever the heck that meant.

"I found him standing hunched up in the corner of the pasture, and brought him in," Lucas added. "I think we should have someone take a look at him fast."

Jodie felt like beating her head against the wall. "Maybe we can have Dr. Eriksson fly in from Vegas?" The vet had his own plane and often flew to the ranch for routine veterinary work. It cost Joe a bundle, but it was the only way he could get services. So far it had worked, because so far there hadn't been a pressing emergency that Mike couldn't handle. No. That had waited until Jodie was here and spineless Mike was gone.

"Already checked. He's on vacation."

"This isn't happening." Jodie rubbed her hands over her face in a gesture of frustration. "What do you suggest?" she asked Lucas.

"I'm no vet, so I suggest we get one."

"Let's go take a look at the bull," she said.

Not that she knew a lot, but Jodie wanted to see how sick the animal was. Two minutes later she had her answer. Real sick. Lucas had herded him into the west end of the barn, opposite the stall where Bronson was recovering, and he was now in a small pen, standing with his body contorted into an oddly hunched position. He either didn't care or was unaware that Jodie and Lucas were there, a few feet away from him. His eyes were half-closed, his breathing labored.

"What are the odds of two emergencies in one week?" she asked in a defeated tone.

Lucas snorted. "On a ranch, it's more like what are the odds of *not* having two emergencies in one week? Your father has been damned lucky so far."

"Well, it's catching up to him now." Jodie patted the metal rail of the enclosure with an air of finality, and then started for the barn door. "I want you to call all the vets within driving distance and see if any will come out here."

"All right." Lucas's tone said it all. No, they wouldn't, and he hated being the guy who had to ask. But he had a better chance at talking them into it than she did.

"Just give it a try, okay?"

"Sure. We're going to need more penicillin for the gelding, too."

"Can you get it at the feed store?" Jodie asked. She was amazed at what the store stocked. Whereas human vaccines were regulated substances, many animal vaccines were readily available to whoever was gutsy enough to give an injection.

"You gotta get it from a vet."

"Figures."

"I'm going to check on the horse before I go back to the house," Jodie told Lucas as he started for the door. Actually, she didn't have the stomach to listen to him get shot down.

The gelding nickered as Jodie approached. "Hi, Bronson."

She and the animal had become close over the past few days. He didn't move much due to pain, but when he saw her coming without Margarite, his ears tipped forward and he limped over within scratching range. Jodie alone meant the itchy spots would be addressed.

"Feeling better?" she asked, rubbing his nose and stroking the thick winter hair on his jowls. As she studied the long crisscrossed lines of sutures across his chest, she felt the now familiar twinge of guilt.

She hadn't asked Sam about the stitches—didn't know if they dissolved or needed to be taken out. Lucas probably knew. He'd better.

"I'll find out about those stitches," she told the gelding. "And when we get them out, you'll be as good as new." Although she doubted her father was going to agree after he saw the poor animal's scarred chest.

Jodie patted the horse and went back to the house. Lucas was still on the phone when she passed through the kitchen into the dining room, his back to her. She'd hoped the local vets would be more receptive to him, but he didn't look like a man who was having a lot of luck.

Five minutes later he walked into the dining room, rubbing a hand over the back of his neck in a helpless gesture. "I can't find a vet."

He left the room as Margarite came through the doorway that led to the living room, broom in hand. The woman stopped dead when she saw the melting globules of snow and mud on the tile floor. Her dark gaze shot to the kitchen entryway just as the door clicked shut.

She let out a breath and started sweeping the snow out of the dining room and into the kitchen. Jodie followed the damp broom trail, glad she'd slipped out of her boots in the mudroom.

"You'd think a man his age would know how to wipe his feet," Margarite grumbled.

"Yeah," she agreed. "But he's here, so maybe we can put up with the mess for a while? You know, just in case another animal needs shots?"

"Yeah, maybe."

Jodie picked up her coat from the chair where she'd tossed it.

"Going somewhere?" Margarite asked.

"I'm going to see Sam Hyatt in person." Even though he'd killed the horse last year, he'd done all right with Bronson. And he was better than no vet at all—although she doubted her father would see things that way.

Margarite shrugged philosophically. "At least that way he can't hang up on you."

KATIE HAD GONE HOME for the day and Sam was deep into the paperwork, hating every minute of it, when Beau came to the clinic.

Sam glanced up at his gangly nephew with a feeling of déjà vu. "Why aren't you at practice?" Beau had passed the test. He should be eligible this week and there was a game on Saturday.

Beau's mouth worked for a moment, poignantly reminding Sam of his brother, Dave, who'd never been good at spitting things out. Now, instead of coaxing his brother into telling him what was going on in his head, he was coaxing Dave's sons into spilling their guts.

"I didn't pass."

"You did. I saw the test."

He'd managed a C, which raised his grade to passing.

"I got turned in for cheating."

Sam's jaw went slack. "Did you cheat?"

Beau looked everywhere but at him.

"Did you?"

"Yeah," he muttered at last.

"You cheated."

"I cheated," Beau said in a stronger voice that almost bordered on a shout. "I didn't understand the problems. I cheated. I need to play."

"Well, you aren't playing now, are you?"

Oh, man. How did he handle this one? Sam wondered. What would his parents have done? They'd experienced the whole gig from diapers through college. He'd been dumped into child rearing during the boys' adolescent stage. Logically, Sam knew that parenting teens wouldn't have been that much easier had he raised the kids from birth, but at least he would have had some experience to fall back on. He could have eased into the traumas of the teens after dealing with small problems like not getting invited to birthday parties or going up the slide backward.

"No," Beau snapped. He gave Sam a frustrated scowl before glancing out the window at the car pulling to a stop in front of the clinic. It wasn't just any car. It was Jodie De Vanti's classic Spitfire, and despite his obvious turmoil, a look of pure envy crossed Beau's face. Sam knew how he felt. A second later Jodie opened the clinic door and Beau took advantage of the moment to make his escape. He hefted his heavy backpack with one hand.

"I'm going to go get something to eat." He nodded at Jodie, then walked around the counter, heading toward the rear exit. Sam watched him go, really wanting to call him back but knowing he had to deal with the rich chick first.

He turned back to Jodie, having no illusions about what prompted this personal call.

"Is this about the bull?" Sam asked, knowing it had to be. Katie had fielded a call from the Barton ranch before she'd gone home.

"Yes."

"Sorry. Can't help you."

Her blue eyes flashed, but her demeanor remained remarkably calm as she said, "Damn it, Sam. I can't have my father's animals dropping like flies."

"Your father got himself into this situation."

"My dad felt justified in bringing suit against you or

he wouldn't have done it...but that's not an excuse," she added, as if remembering her mission was to finesse him, not beat him in an argument. "Just an explanation."

"Feeling justified and *being* justified are not the same," Sam felt obliged to point out. "Or maybe it is for you legal types."

"We legal types understand the difference," she said patiently, even though she was obviously annoyed at his remark. "He lost a thirty-thousand-dollar horse. Surely you can understand—"

"The horse couldn't have been saved."

"The professor from the UC Davis disagreed, which was why my father brought suit." She met Sam's eyes, her expression candid. "You can't fault him for that. He sought the opinion of an expert and acted on that opinion."

Ah, yes. The star witness, who'd been working with twenty-twenty hindsight and after-the-fact information.

"Your expert didn't convince the judge, did he?" Sam reminded her. And the expert hadn't been there the night the horse died, either. Sam had been, working his ass off trying to save an animal with a twisted gut. And he'd done everything he could, everything he'd been capable of...although it had happened only a few weeks after Dave's death and Sam had still been suffering from shock. Hadn't been thinking all that straight. But he'd gone over his responses a thousand times in his mind, logically reviewing what he'd known at the time.

He hadn't made a mistake, and he truly resented Joe for coming after him at such a time in his life.

"No," Jodie agreed.

"Because I was right," he replied. And it felt good to say that out loud to a Barton. He put his palms on the counter that separated them and leaned closer. "And that is why you can't get services. People don't want to deal with your family."

JODIE FOUGHT BOTH desperation and exasperation, with a healthy dose of anger thrown in. Why was she wasting her time here? She wasn't going to win and the bull was going to die.

She put her own hands on the counter opposite Sam's and leaned across the laminate surface until they were practically nose to nose. "*I* didn't sue you," she said adamantly. "*I'm* asking for help. Not my father."

Sam wasn't buying her argument. Hell, even she wasn't buying it. She'd sat in court with her dad, which made her pretty much a party to the action, even if she hadn't been the one to file suit.

"I am not going to be responsible for killing my father's prize bull."

"He killed his bull," Sam said stubbornly. "Not you."

"The animal is still alive, Sam. You could keep him that way." She'd barely gotten the last word out of her mouth when the phone rang.

Sam glanced at the caller ID. "It's my nephew. I have to take this."

"*Will* you come to the ranch?" Jodie asked before

he got the receiver to his ear, and was horrified to hear a tiny crack in her otherwise even voice. What next? Sobs?

Instead of answering her, Sam said into the receiver, "What is it, Ty?" He bent his head as he listened.

Jodie knew she'd hit her breaking point then. Her mission was futile. The bull was going to die. Her father would come home to a dead animal and missing a vet-trained cowboy. His blood pressure would skyrocket. The vacation would end up being wasted time….

Not on her watch.

"Thanks so much, Sam," she said sarcastically, glad that her voice remained strong even as her eyes started to burn. "You probably would have killed the bull, anyway," she muttered, too low for him to hear.

She turned and walked out the door before she did something both embarrassing and useless like bursting into tears. She felt them building, ready to seep out of the corners of her eyes, but they were tears of frustration and anger, not of self-pity. One spilled down her cheek, fueling her anger, as she yanked open the door to the Spitfire. She wiped it away with a jerky swipe of her gloved hand, muttered a single socially unacceptable word, then started the car.

She could see Sam through the window, still behind the counter where she'd left him, watching her drive away. It was all she could do not to flip him off. She made another swipe at her damp cheeks with the back of her hand.

She wasn't done. Not by a long shot. But she had to do something fast, and dithering around with Sam wasn't going to cure her sick cow. Bull. Whatever. She'd wasted a lot of time coming here, but at least she knew now that she wasn't going to be dealing with Sam anymore. The guy was impossible. And hardhearted.

Her next step was to drive the fifty miles down to Otto and meet with Stan Stewart, the vet there. Lucas had already talked to him on the phone, but maybe she could finagle a deal with him in person. They'd danced before at a social function in Otto and he hadn't seemed exactly immune to her. Perhaps one on one…

Jodie pulled into the gas station two blocks from Sam's clinic and got out of the car, wishing she'd fueled up at the ranch. But she hadn't thought of it in her hurry to get to town and try to rustle up some medical help. She slipped her credit card into the slot, punched the buttons, then almost kicked the machine as the computerized gizmo took its own sweet time validating her card. Finally, gasoline started flowing into her tank.

She leaned back against the side of her dark blue car, not caring for once if she scratched the paint, and pressed her gloved palm to her forehead, feeling the heat of her flushed skin through the thin leather. A truck pulled to a stop on the other side of the pump and Sam got out. Jodie's mouth almost dropped open.

"Did I leave before you were done lambasting my family?" she snapped, even as a small part of her wondered if she might regret the words.

His mouth tightened ominously at her sarcastic tone and Jodie made an effort to control herself. "I don't have your cell number, so I couldn't call you," he said.

"Why would you need to?"

Sam shifted his weight self-consciously. "Do you want me to phone Stan Stewart and see if he'd be willing to examine your bull?"

Jodie frowned suspiciously. This was a big about-face. "May I ask why you'd do that?" The numbers on the gas pump whirled by. Her baby was thirsty.

"Because I hate seeing animals die just because they have the misfortune of being owned by an asshole." There was not an iota of apology in his voice.

Jodie met his eyes, which looked almost silver in the fluorescent lighting above the gas pump. There was more to it than that. She had the oddest feeling he felt sorry for her. But as much as she hated that, she was more than willing to go with it. Anything to keep that flipping bull alive—if it wasn't already too late.

"I'd appreciate it if you did that." The words came out stiffly.

The pump mechanism clicked off and Jodie removed the spout from her tank, slapping the nozzle back into place.

Sam pulled his cell phone out of his pocket and pressed a single button. A moment later he was talking. Jodie wrapped her arms around her middle, focusing on the oil stained concrete beneath her feet as she waited for a verdict and tried to keep from tapping her toe. Less than thirty seconds into the conversation, she knew the answer would not be in her favor.

Deep breaths. Deep, deep breaths.

Sam clicked the phone shut. "Stan can't make it."

Jodie didn't say a word. What could she say?

Her mouth tightened as she studied the ground at her

feet for another few seconds, trying to come up with an alternative plan to save the poor animal that was going to die because her father was an asshole.

"I'll take a look at the bull. Unless you're afraid I'll kill him."

Jodie's eyes flashed up. "I'll pay you well," she replied automatically.

"Damned right you will."

CHAPTER FOUR

SAM DROVE HOME, knowing for a fact he'd lost his mind. Okay, he needed the money—as would anyone with oversize eating machines in their home—and he honestly hated to let any creature die. But he could have talked Stan into driving up to the ranch tomorrow. Deep in his gut Sam knew the real reason he was going was because he felt for Jodie.

Crazy. But it had also been crazy to see a woman who'd quite possibly never owned a pet in her life arguing passionately for him to come save a bull. More than that, though, he'd gotten a sense of something else…a sense that Jodie truly dreaded her father coming home and finding the bull dead. She'd been on the edge of desperation, trying to hold back tears.

He felt sorry for Jodie De Vanti. Go figure.

"You're coming with me," Sam said to Beau as soon as he got back home to switch his personal truck for the utility one.

"Where're we going?"

"To the Barton ranch."

"But…" One look at his uncle and Beau shut his mouth.

They rode most of the thirty miles in tense silence.

Sam still wasn't certain how he was going to handle this cheating situation, but he wanted Beau to be available when he figured it out. Yes, he was probably overreacting, but what if he screwed up raising these guys? He owed it to his brother to do it right.

What would you do, Dave? How about a nudge in the right direction…?

"What's the case?" Beau finally asked.

"Sick bull."

"Oh." Another long silence ensued.

Finally Sam couldn't hold in the question any longer. Even though he knew the answer, he had to ask. "Why'd you cheat on the math test?"

"Because I wanted to play."

"I'm glad they caught you."

"Everybody does it," Beau grumbled.

Sam at last understood why parents asked their kids, "If everyone jumped off a bridge, would you do it, too?" He'd just come damned close to saying those exact words.

His nephew shot him a look when Sam didn't reply. "I know it doesn't make it right."

"More than that, it makes it so I can't trust you."

"You can trust me."

Sam's jaw tightened. "Cheating on a test is the same as lying. I don't trust people who lie."

Beau looked as though he wanted to argue the point, but after a few seconds he turned to stare out the window when Sam drove onto the wide gravel road leading to the Barton property. They passed under the arched metal sign announcing the Zephyr Valley Ranch. Sam would always think of the spread as Boggy Flats, its original name, but a guy like Joe Barton wouldn't live on a place called that. The locals still smirked about the name Zephyr Valley.

Jodie was waiting for Sam on the steps of the glassed-in back porch, hands shoved in the pockets of her coat, her body held stiffly, though whether from cold or nerves, Sam had no idea. She stepped out onto the freshly shoveled path as the truck slowed, and walked briskly to the barn. By the time he parked she was waiting for him next to the door.

"Grab the kit," he said to Beau before getting out of the truck. Jodie watched him approach, then opened the door and preceded him inside. The barn was wonderfully warm and smelled of fresh straw, animals and earth. Most people could barely afford to heat their houses this winter and Joe had a toasty barn. Sam had to appreciate that.

"The bull's down here," Jodie said, all business as she motioned toward the paneled corrals at the back of the huge building. Sure enough, a handsome Gelbvieh bull stood hunched in a pen filled with clean straw, his head down. He didn't move when they approached.

"How long's he been like this?"

"Since this morning. Lucas found him in the pasture and brought him in."

"Lucas Reynolds?" It couldn't be. Joe had fired Lucas's ass last fall, but Sam couldn't really blame him, much as he'd like to. Lucas's drinking made him unreliable.

"Yes. He's been through rehab, so I decided to give him another chance."

"Where's Mike? Still on vacation?"

Jodie cleared her throat. "Mike, uh, quit." Sam was not surprised. When the guy had a few at Fuzzy's Tavern, he tended to unload about how much Joe rode him. "Lucas was back in town, so...I hired him."

Sam bet she couldn't find any other help. "Is he around?"

"No." She bit her lip and Sam noticed just how done in she looked. It had been a rugged few days for her.

"You really can't keep help, can you?" he said drily as he climbed the panel rails and stepped down into the pen.

"Lucas has a meeting he has to attend, but he took a ranch cell phone if you need to talk to him."

"Alcoholics Anonymous?"

"As a matter of fact, yes."

Sam didn't have a lot of use for drunks, even those he'd known most of his life. He'd been robbed of a brother by a drunk. But this was the first time Lucas had gone to rehab, the first time he'd admitted he had a problem with alcohol, as far as Sam knew.

"I don't think I'll have to talk to him." All the information he needed was standing there before him, having difficulty breathing.

Beau came in then with the kit in one hand, looking at the ground as he walked, scuffling his big feet. Sam collected his instruments, then climbed over the panels and approached the lethargic bull. The animal barely moved when Sam ran his hand over the brisket, checking for fluid accumulation before taking vitals. From the way the bull was standing hunched up, Sam had a strong suspicion of what the problem was. He just hoped the cure would be simple and not involve a rumenotomy.

"How long have you had this bull?" he asked Jodie, who was watching his every move intently from the other side of the rails. He only half expected her to know, but she answered without hesitation.

"He was shipped up from Oklahoma just before my parents left. Dad was really happy to get him…which is why he can't die while I'm in charge."

"You didn't make him sick," Sam replied with a touch of impatience.

"No." But she didn't sound convinced, which Sam found telling. No wonder Joe couldn't keep help if his own daughter had trouble dealing with him.

"What'll your dad do if the animal does die? Besides sue me."

"He's not going to sue you," Jodie snapped. "And…I just don't want him to come back from Europe and have to deal with stuff like…bulls dying. That kind of defeats the purpose of the vacation."

"Probably does," Sam agreed, wondering for a moment what it felt like to take an honest to goodness vacation. It'd probably be a decade or two before he found out.

JODIE WATCHED as Sam ran his hands over the bull, squeezing the top of the animal's shoulders, making him hunch up even more. But when the vet pulled out a syringe to draw a blood sample, she suddenly felt the need to check on Bronson. She'd ask Sam about the stitches when he was done. The horse's stall was only a few yards away, so she'd still be within talking range if Sam had something important to say, like, "Oh, all he needs is a shot and he'll be good as new."

Sam's son was already at the stall, stroking the horse. He was subdued and Jodie wondered if he and Sam had argued about something on the way out. Sam was tense and the kid was sullen.

"How's it going?" she asked as the teen patted the horse's neck. He had the same gray eyes, the same angular face as Sam. He was going to be a heartbreaker, if he wasn't already.

"Good." Conversation over.

"Are you going to be a vet, too?"

"Only if it doesn't involve any math." The boy spoke more to himself than to her.

She glanced over her shoulder at Sam, who was drawing blood from a vein in the bull's neck, then quickly turned her head away, feeling the familiar churning in her stomach. Blood and a needle. Double whammy.

"Don't like blood?" the kid asked.

"Not a fan," Jodie agreed, seeing no reason to lie about the obvious. He seemed to find that mildly amusing. "How about you?" she asked.

"It doesn't bother me." He sent her a sidelong glance, looking as though he was going to say something else, but then changed his mind.

Sam climbed over the rails then, rattling the panels and drawing their attention. Jodie quickly walked over to find him packing away the samples.

"Is he going to be all right?" she asked when he didn't offer an immediate prognosis.

"I don't know," Sam said, meeting her eyes candidly. "I'll have more of an idea after I run the blood."

"Are you doing everything? I mean, expense is not an issue." Maybe she shouldn't have said that. His eyes flashed as if she'd insulted his intelligence, which she probably had.

"I'm doing everything."

What she saw in his face made her believe him. Okay. She couldn't buy a cure.

She watched the bull for a few seconds, willing him to get better. Now.

"I've given him antibiotics, and as soon as I get the lab results, I'll be back."

"How far away is the lab?" she asked. How long was this going to take?

"The local hospital."

"Really." Jodie blinked at him. "It must be interesting if they ever mix up blood work." One corner of Sam's mouth quirked up in a way she might have found interesting if her stomach wasn't tied in a knot. "Will you come out tomorrow and check on him even if you don't have results?"

"Yeah." He didn't seem thrilled about the idea, but he'd accepted the case and was obviously going to see it through. He looked at the stall where the kid was still petting Bronson, and called, "Beau! Time to leave."

The teen headed to the door without saying a word, reinforcing Jodie's impression that something wasn't quite right between him and Sam.

"I didn't realize you had a son," she said as the door swung shut. A son usually indicated the presence of a wife, yet Sam wore no ring.

"He's my nephew."

Ah. "He resembles you."

"I know." The words came out in a way that made Jodie feel vaguely foolish for having made the observation.

"I'll go get the checkbook." She'd had enough of this conversation.

"Make it a hundred even, for now."

WHEN SAM GOT INTO THE RIG, Beau was already slumped down in the seat, staring sullenly at the dashboard. Sam ignored him and started the engine, pulling up close to the steps so Jodie didn't have far to go when she came back out to hand him the payment through the open window. Again he was struck by how exhausted she looked. And how vulnerable. He was certain she had no idea or the lawyer mask would have slipped back into place.

"Thank you for coming." Her words were spoken in a clipped, formal tone.

"See you tomorrow," Sam replied automatically. Beau continued to stare straight ahead and Sam could only imagine what Jodie thought of his giant pouting nephew.

She went back in the house, and as Sam folded the

check to tuck it away in his shirt pocket, he noticed that she'd added some on account. Jodie De Vanti was either grateful or trying to buy herself a vet—a vet who'd better damned well be able to successfully treat the bull or he'd be dealing with Joe when he got home. Sam had no illusions there, but that wasn't his biggest concern at the moment.

No brilliant solutions for the cheating problem had popped into his brain while he was working, other than grounding his nephew's ass forever. He'd hoped that he and Beau could talk on the drive home, but it was obvious there would be no conversation tonight. The kid needed time to cool off, to realize that the world wasn't against him and maybe he had something to do with the jam he was in.

Dave? Sam sent out another plea for help. *Ideas?*

Nothing.

He missed his brother.

Sam drove through the dark countryside, wondering how this was going to play out, trying to convince himself that it would be okay, that this wasn't the beginning of Beau embarking on a life of crime. Logically, Sam knew it wasn't, but the parenting game brought a whole lot of "what ifs" with it.

He loved his nephews more than life, but sometimes he couldn't help but reminisce about how simple his life had been prior to his brother's death.

SAM WAS INVITED TO A meeting at Beau's school the Friday following the cheating incident. At home Beau was grounded for at least two weeks, and Sam planned on working the kid's butt off around the clinic. Now they would be informed of the academic and sports-related consequences.

The meeting was a quick one, since it took place just before class started, and the group—Mr. Domingo, the principal; Mr. Gerard, the basketball coach; and Miss Simms, the math teacher—agreed to a two-game suspension. After that, Beau could play if his grades were passing. Since he'd received a zero for the math test, that was going to be difficult, and he knew it.

He stared glumly at the floor for much of the meeting, making Sam want to reiterate once again that the only reason his nephew was there was because he'd made a stupid choice. But Sam had already said that at least five or six times that morning and the message did not seem to be sinking in.

"I want you home immediately after practice," Sam said when Beau got up to leave. "No hanging with the guys."

Beau nodded, his expression blank, and then disappeared out the door. Sam could almost feel his nephew's relief at finally escaping. The principal muttered something about having to patrol the halls, and followed Beau out of the room. Gerard disappeared after him.

"Beau's a good kid," Miss Simms said, directing her attention back to Sam.

"I know. I want to make sure he stays that way."

"You'd be surprised how many kids cheat. Even the good ones."

Frustration welled up inside Sam. "It's not acceptable."

"No," she agreed mildly. "It's not. But it's not the end of the world. He got caught. I'm certain he'll have consequences at home." No doubt. "Right now we need to see that he understands math."

Okay, was she politely telling him to get a grip? Quite possibly. But she wasn't in charge of seeing that her dead brother's children got off on the right foot in life.

"Any clues how to do that?"

"Small steps. Beau has trouble focusing, and when he gets frustrated he shuts down." Miss Simms craned her neck to see if the hall outside the office was clear, then continued speaking in a tone just above a whisper. "Coach Gerard has tried to help him, since he's also a math teacher, but frankly, he assumes too much understanding. Beau needs to be taken slowly from step one when he encounters a new concept. To be reminded of what he's learned before and told how to apply it. Some kids make an instant leap. Others need review."

"Does Beau have a learning disability?"

"He has a different learning pattern. What works for the majority of kids doesn't work so well for him. He can come in during the mornings and I'll help him."

"He hasn't been doing that?" Sam asked. Beau was supposed to be.

The math teacher gave Sam a weary smile. "He usually comes by on the morning of the test, panicked."

Another topic Sam needed to address with his nephew. He felt stupid for not already being aware.

"I ordered a book online," he said. "I'll try to help him more."

"Feel free to call on me."

Sam forced a smile. "Thank you. I appreciate the offer." It would have been great if Miss Simms had known of a tutor, but all she could recommend were peer tutors. Sam didn't believe another kid was up to the job of hammering math into Beau's head when adults couldn't get the job done.

He left the office and stepped into the milling swarms of kids in the hall. He caught sight of Beau standing next to a locker, talking to Marisa Brown, the perkiest of perky cheerleaders, and resisted the urge to push his way through the crowd and tell him he needed to focus on school, not women.

Instead Sam continued to follow a stream of kids until he got to the exit. He'd fight that battle, along with several others, tonight. Right now he wanted to get his first call—the Barton ranch—over and done with.

JODIE GOT UP EARLY and checked the bull—thankfully he wasn't belly up—then sat at the kitchen table, sipping coffee and staring out the picture window at the snowy fields with the pastel-blue mountains behind them.

She was grateful Sam had come the night before, grateful that he was doing what he could...but this was her father's prize bull. She had to do everything *she* could, so she'd put in another call to Eriksson's office, hoping to leave a message on voice mail for a call back. Instead she got the same recording as the time she'd called for advice about Bronson. Dr. Eriksson was out of the office for yet another week.

What kind of vet took *two*-week vacations? Didn't he realize that people needed him? Now?

"Lucas said Sam is coming back this morning," Margarite said as she sat down on the other side of the table with a crossword puzzle book and a cup of tea.

"Yes."

"Thank goodness. I don't want your dad to blame Lucas if the bull dies." She spoke offhandedly, opening the book and finding where she'd left off, but her words made Jodie's temples throb.

"The bull isn't going to die."

"All the same..." Margarite said in an unconvinced tone.

My father won't blame Lucas. He's more reasonable than that.

Jodie looked back out the window, the words unspoken. Margarite was no one's fool. She lived on the ranch full-time and saw things Jodie didn't. But that didn't mean she was interpreting them correctly.

"Lucas hasn't been here long enough to be responsible," Jodie finally said. "I'll make sure my dad knows the truth. And since Lucas did me a favor and came back, I'll do my best to see that Dad keeps him on...if he wants to stay, that is." Granted, her father wasn't a big believer in second chances, but he would listen to reason—especially economic reason. And if no other local person would work for him during the winter months, as both Mike and Margarite intimated, keeping Lucas made sense.

"Good luck," the housekeeper said in a way that made Jodie feel oddly weary. Her dad had developed one heck of a rep with people who just didn't get how he operated. People who didn't see how much he had accomplished in life through strength of character and his no-excuses attitude. "Is Sam going to be on call if Lucas needs help when the heifers calve?"

"Is he likely to need help?" Jodie certainly hoped not. She'd been so damned fortunate to get Sam to come out here as many times as she had. It seemed unlikely that her luck would hold.

Margarite looked up after fitting a few letters into the puzzle. "You do know that heifers are first-time mothers, right?"

"Yes." One of the few bits of cattle knowledge she had.

"Well, because of that, it takes them longer to come back into season after they give birth, so they're bred to calve early. That gives them time to get pregnant again. The bad part is that it's colder and nastier when they have their babies. Plus they have weaker calves and less colostrum, so, yes, there's a good chance we'll need a vet."

"Wonderful."

"On the bright side, it's not muddy, so there're not as many cases of scours."

Jodie had no idea what Margarite was talking about, and she didn't ask for clarification. The word *scours* had an ominous ring to it.

"Joe's been at this for three years, so he understands the reality, but…"

"He's a businessman," Jodie finished for her. He would want a live calf by the side of every cow. Profit for each investment.

"Lucas can handle regular births, but he can't do C-sections." Margarite knocked on the wooden table. "Not that we'll have any."

Jodie smiled weakly and stared back out at the line of cattle stretched across the snowy pasture, heads down, eating the hay Lucas had dropped.

Would her father want Sam on the ranch on a regular basis?

No.

Would Sam agree to come on a regular basis?

Probably not—unless the money was a sure thing.

Was she feeling an edge of desperation?

Definitely.

"Hey, you're fortunate none of those fancy mares Joe bought last summer are due to foal until spring," Margarite said, breaking into Jodie's thoughts. "You'll be long gone by then." She picked up her pencil again just as Sam's distinctive bronze-colored truck appeared on the crest of a small hill about a half mile away.

Jodie watched the vehicle disappear into the dip half a mile from the house. "Margarite?"

The housekeeper looked up.

"Is Sam a good vet?"

"Yeah. He is."

Jodie did her best to keep an open mind, which wasn't easy after hearing her father rant about Sam for months. "Did he make a mistake with my dad's horse?"

Margarite hesitated, then said, "I'm not a vet, so I can't say."

A politically correct and totally unhelpful answer. Jodie went to the sink and rinsed her cup, setting it on the drain board before going out into the mudroom and putting on her barn coat. She wound a red silk scarf around her neck and went outside into the nippy mid-morning air to wait for Sam.

Mike Bower had better darned well hope that she never accidentally ran into him, because if she did, she was going to indulge in some retribution for putting her in her current position. Sam might or might not be a good vet, but she felt decidedly uncomfortable being in a position where she was beholden to him.

CHAPTER FIVE

Have some answers. Please have some answers.

Sam parked beside the pump house and went straight to the barn without acknowledging her, so Jodie crossed the wide drive to find out what was happening.

He was in the bull's pen, doing something with the big animal when she opened the door. She stepped inside, but hung back, not sure what he was up to or if it involved blood and gore. Bronson knocked his hoof against the stall door and Jodie went to see if Lucas had fed him yet. He hadn't, so she put a flake of hay in the manger and then went in with the fork to clean the pen. She was spreading straw, shaking the flakes with the fork to loosen them, when Sam approached.

"How's the bull?" she asked, standing straight, both hands gripping the pitchfork.

"I think he'll get better now. If he doesn't, I'll have to operate."

"What's wrong with him?" Jodie was focusing on the "get better" part. There was hope.

"I suspect traumatic reticuloperitonitis."

"Which is?" *A big long vet word.* She hoped he wasn't trying to dazzle her with smoke and mirrors and vocabulary.

"Hardware disease. I think he swallowed metal, like a nail or wire, and it's perforating his rumen."

"He what? Where would he get a nail?"

"Feed. Cattle don't chew. They swallow all kinds of stuff."

"My dad isn't going to believe this one."

"If he continues in the ranching business, he will."

"What's the treatment if you don't operate? I mean… it's a nail. That can't be good."

"I fed him a magnet."

"Very funny."

Sam's expression didn't change. "It's the treatment. Look it up on the Web." He seemed pretty damned confident. "The magnet will pull the nail out of the rumen wall and the wall will heal if all goes well."

"Do you make this up?" Jodie asked.

"Would I risk another lawsuit?"

Probably not, and she felt a ridiculous urge to trust him. "Okay. You feed him a magnet. How do you get the magnet out? Does it just…come out naturally?"

Sam shook his head. "Cattle aren't set up like that. The magnet stays in there."

"Forever?" This didn't sound right.

"Yeah. It doesn't hurt the bull and the metal sticking to it can't perforate anything vital. Sometimes we have to feed an animal two magnets during its life if one gets too much stuff stuck to it."

Jodie heard the theme to the *Twilight Zone* playing in her head. "But you don't know that it's…hardware whatever. Shouldn't you x-ray or do an ultrasound or something before jamming a magnet down the bull's throat?"

"X-ray on an animal as massive as that bull only picks up large objects. Ultrasound is generally useless, and even if it isn't hardware disease, the magnet won't hurt him." Sam fixed cool gray eyes on her face. "I'm doing what I can. If the bull doesn't respond, I'll make an incision, feel around and see if I can find anything."

Jodie's stomach flip-flopped at the mental image of Sam "feeling around" a cow's insides.

He shifted the medical kit from one hand to the other, making her wonder how heavy it was. "My next call is fifty miles from here, so I need to get going."

Jodie followed him out of the barn, debating with herself. *Ask him? Don't ask him?* He was stowing the kit in a compartment of the utility truck when she made her decision. "If we have trouble with calving, can I call you?"

He turned toward her, looking at her in a way that made her nerves tingle. His eyes were the same color as a winter sky with a storm moving in. She cleared her throat before continuing.

"I've been talking to Margarite and she told me early calving would start soon. Mike was supposed to be here, to handle the difficult births."

"And Mike isn't."

"No. He isn't. If you'll agree to be on call for the calving, I'll pay a retainer."

"What if you don't use my services?"

"That's a chance I'll have to take." Sam just looked

at her. "So," she said briskly. "What do you say?" She actually felt her heart start to beat faster as she waited for his reply.

Sam ran a hand over his jaw. The stubble there was reddish-brown, much darker than his blond hair. He was going to agree. Jodie could feel it.

"The minute your dad comes back, I'm off the job. He can get his own help."

"Agreed." Jodie had no other choice. Calves were coming.

JODIE DID INDEED PAY SAM a healthy retainer when he returned to the ranch the next morning, and he in turn handed her a legal document, one that let him off the hook in case of any mishaps, including the two animals he'd already treated. She read through it and then signed without hesitation. Margarite witnessed the signature in Joe's office.

Sam had had the paper drawn up shortly after winning the lawsuit, and for a while he'd used it with new customers. During the last several months, though, it had sat untouched in his file cabinet, but now it was out and back in action. He was fairly certain that a sharp lawyer would find ways around it, which might be why Jodie had signed so readily, but it made him feel slightly better working on the Barton ranch.

"I researched hardware disease," Jodie said conversationally after she'd made a copy of the document. She seemed less stressed now that he'd agreed to provide emergency care, and maybe that was why he was having such a hard time keeping his eyes off her. He'd seen her as the cool, efficient lawyer, and he'd seen her angry, desperate and determined. But he'd never encountered this warm, approachable Jodie. "I guess magnets are the therapy, although it sounds whacked to me."

"Yes, whacked," Sam repeated solemnly, for want of anything better to say.

Jodie fought a smile, but it broke through as she made a note on the top of the document, and Sam felt an unexpected jolt of desire through his body.

Where had that come from?

Probably from not having sex in a really long time.

Between running the business and monitoring the boys, he didn't seem to have a lot of free time on his hands. Dating had been one of the things that had fallen by the wayside as he struggled to keep up with being a vet, business owner and parent.

Frankly, he missed having a social life, but in two years his life would be back. Kind of. He was beginning to understand that parenting never ended.

Jodie was still half smiling when she set the pen she'd used back in a fancy-schmancy carved holder, and Sam did not like the effect it was having on him.

"I'm going to take the stitches out of the horse's chest. Want to watch?"

Jodie's smile instantly faded and she shook her head. "No. Thank you. Just tell me how the bull is doing before you go."

"I'll tell Lucas." Sam didn't particularly want to see Jodie again before he left.

"That works." She gave him a long speculative

look before opening a file drawer and slipping the contract into a folder, making him wonder what she was thinking.

Probably best if he didn't know, just as it was best that she never find out what he'd been thinking.

Sam went to the barn, checked the bull—which appeared less lethargic now that the magnet was drawing the nail or wire out of the ruminant wall—and then removed the stitches from the horse's chest. He was pleased with how well the area was healing. There'd be visible scars, but they weren't nearly as ugly as they could have been; in fact, with a growth of winter coat, they'd barely be noticeable. He'd done a decent job in spite of the shaky light and numbing cold. Joe wouldn't see it that way, of course, but screw him.

Sam found Lucas fueling up the tractor, and told him the bull was improving and that the horse could go back out into the pasture. It was the first time Sam could remember the guy not reeking of alcohol.

"Jodie said I can call you for help with the difficult calves?" His breath crystallized in the cold air.

"Yeah."

"Why?" Lucas asked point-blank.

"Because Joe isn't here and I need the money."

Lucas looked back at the bull. "Same reason I'm here. I don't suppose you need any help around the clinic come spring?"

"I have the boys, and even if I did need help, I couldn't pay you."

Lucas nodded. He reached up to adjust the faded yellow silk scarf that protected his neck, then took the fuel nozzle out of the tractor's gas tank.

"But give me a call anyway," Sam said, feeling for the guy. It had to be rough, starting your life over in your early sixties. "You never know. Maybe I'll win the lottery or something."

FOR ONCE THE Zephyr Valley Ranch was experiencing a zephyr rather than a fierce north wind. The warm breeze blew for two days, melting most of the snow and creating a quagmire in the pastures. Lucas was having trouble feeding the animals without getting the tractor stuck, but so far had managed to get the big machine back to the barn every morning.

"This'll be followed by a freeze and two feet of snow," Lucas predicted. "Just in time for the first calves. I don't know what it is about freezing cold, but it makes cows give birth."

"Wonderful," Jodie said, but she wasn't as concerned now as she had been a week ago. Sam had cashed the retainer check, so she knew he'd be at the ranch when called, ready to save the day. Her father would not be thrilled when he discovered that he'd not only lost all his hired help, but had regained two that he'd fired. However, drastic times called for drastic measures. Jodie's goal was to make certain as many animals were alive when he came home as when he'd left.

With five weeks of his vacation to go, she was beginning to hope that maybe her father would arrive before the early calving. Lucas assured her there was no way that was going to happen. Calves were coming, probably within a week. But on a positive note, the sick bull was eating again and had regained his strength, to the point that Lucas had put him back out in the bachelor pasture with the other bulls. Another crisis averted, thanks to Sam. Jodie was going to owe him a huge debt of gratitude if things continued as they were, and right now she owed him a debt of the monetary variety. Lucas had picked up more penicillin and some amazingly expensive colostrum from the clinic yesterday, and Jodie decided to pay the bill when she went into Wesley for a few personal odds and ends. With the warm wind still blowing, it was too nice to stay in the house.

There were no cars in the parking spaces in front of the clinic, and no one behind the counter. Jodie called a hello. No reply. Odd. She waited a few minutes, and then leaned over the counter to set the check beside the computer keyboard.

Next stop the library. She was almost to her car when she heard the distinctive sound of a basketball hitting concrete somewhere behind the clinic, a sound that always gave her an adrenaline rush. It was followed by male voices, one of them Sam's. Jodie reversed course.

Did Sam play basketball? He was certainly tall enough, and the thought of Sam driving hard for the goal...*oh, yeah*. She followed the path around the clinic to the yard that separated the building from Sam's house. He and two boys stood on a concrete pad under a portable basketball hoop, and were in the middle of a heated discussion. Sam had the ball tucked under one arm and a finger in the air when he caught sight of Jodie. He stopped talking and both boys turned to follow his gaze, their expressions—and features—identical.

Sam had twin nephews.

"I just dropped off the check," Jodie said, her eyes moving from one tall, fair-haired kid to the other before settling back on their uncle. Maybe it was because there were three of them that she was struck by how good-looking they were. "It's beside the keyboard."

"Thanks," Sam said, bouncing the ball. The nephew Jodie hadn't previously met reached out and expertly snagged it away from him before making a lazy layup.

"I win," he said.

"In your dreams," Sam replied.

"Yeah? Well, I could take you and Beau together." He made a sweeping gesture. "Or all three of you," he said cockily, including Jodie in the competition.

"How about plain old two-on-two?" Jodie asked. Her request was immediately followed by three superior masculine smirks, as if they thought she was kidding. She wasn't. In her busy life not many opportunities arose for a pickup game these days, but when she'd been in school… "Me and Beau against…" She gestured at the other nephew.

"Tyler," he said, passing the ball from hand to hand.

"Tyler and Sam."

"Yeah," Tyler agreed with a wide grin, palming the ball. Beau looked less than enthused. Sam said nothing, but he was looking at Jodie as if trying to figure her angle.

"What do you say, Beau?" Tyler jerked his head at Sam, and Beau's expression changed.

He gave a shrug. "Why not?"

Tyler tossed Jodie the ball. She passed to Beau, who went in for an easy layup, with Ty and Sam giving little defense. She had a feeling this was Sam's way of spotting them a few points. That wasn't the way Jodie played. When Tyler passed the ball in to Sam, Jodie went chest to chest with him, waving her arms and keeping him cornered. She rather enjoyed the expressions that crossed his face when he realized that, despite her height disadvantage, she was playing for real.

"Come on, Sam!" Tyler called.

Finally Sam made a bounce pass to Tyler, who maneuvered around his brother and took a shot. Rim ball. Jodie rebounded, pivoted, dribbled, shot for two. Then she took her place next to Sam, ready to guard. She pushed the hair out of her eyes with one hand, while extending the other toward Sam's midsection.

Tyler and Beau exchanged looks.

"I didn't know you were a player," Sam said close to her ear. Tingles went up her spine.

"I'm a player," she replied. Joe Barton's daughter didn't play sissy ball. She'd been the season MVP three years in a row during high school.

Tyler passed the ball to Sam and the game was on.

The guys were each a good five inches taller than her five foot seven, but she was fast and agile. Ball handling had been her forte, and the moves came back automatically.

Tyler and Sam won by one point, but neither Beau

nor Jodie were disappointed with their efforts. Beau held out his hand for a high five and Jodie jumped to smack his palm.

"Where'd you learn to play?" he asked, smiling at her in a way that made her very aware of him, of her, of the possibilities they could explore.

"High school. I played varsity for three years." Joe had been disappointed it hadn't been four. When she'd made the JV—junior varsity—team as a freshman, she'd been proud, since the competition was fierce, but immediately realized that her father had expected more. She'd worked like crazy that year and over the summer to make varsity, and had been rewarded with a proud father. And when she'd won MVP…terrifically proud father.

"We're going out for burgers tonight," Beau said. "Want to come?"

Jodie couldn't help but feel honored to be invited, since she was certain these boys had heard a lot of bad things about her family.

"Oh, I, uh…really can't. I bought groceries for Margarite and need to get them home. She's baking for a bake sale." Jodie was surprised at how disappointed the boys looked.

"Well, maybe another time," Beau said with a charming smile that came close to swaying her. He was so different than he'd been the night he'd accompanied Sam to the ranch. Whatever problem they'd been having had apparently blown over…which made her wonder what kind of problem an uncle and nephew could have that was so serious. They'd acted much more like father and son.

"How's the bull?" Sam asked after the boys had started toward the house. The jeans he wore accentuated his long legs a whole lot more than the canvas coveralls he'd had on every time he'd visited the ranch.

"Lucas put him back in the pasture today."

"Excellent." Sam bounced the ball a couple times. "How'd you become such a good basketball player?"

"Same way anyone does. I spent a lot of hours on the court."

"I never took you for an athlete."

"Why?"

"I don't know. You just seem so...girlie."

"Girlie." She echoed the word flatly, not at all flattered by the assessment. Feminine maybe, but girlie?

Sam shifted his weight, but his eyes stayed locked on hers when he said, "I mean that in a good way."

"Do you?" she asked, noting that though his gaze was direct, the color had risen in his cheeks. Was Sam Hyatt shy? She found the thought intriguing and was debating how she could test her hypothesis when the door to the house opened and his nephews came out wearing gray hooded sweatshirts, one emblazoned with University of Nevada Reno Wolf Pack across the chest and the other with UNLV Running Rebels. All the bases covered.

"Can I drive your car sometime?" Tyler asked.

"No." Sam spoke firmly. Jodie was glad, because it saved her from having to do so.

"Well," she said, "have fun. I'll see you guys later." She picked her way over the half-frozen grass to the path at the side of the clinic.

Jodie drove home thinking about Sam and his boys, but mainly about Sam. Handsome man. Good ball handler. Possibly shy. The snap of attraction she felt when they were together was...energizing. And so was the game. She smiled with satisfaction as she turned onto the Zephyr Ranch road. All in all, not a bad trip to town.

Her dad would have a fit if he knew she was entertaining carnal thoughts about Sam. Oh, well. She smiled again.

"I thought you'd be back sooner," Margarite commented as she helped Jodie carry the bags in from the garage.

"I got waylaid at Sam's place."

Her eyebrows rose.

"Pick-up game." Margarite's eyebrows remained in an elevated position, and Jodie realized the housekeeper had no idea what she was talking about. "I played basketball with him and his nephews."

"Oh." Margarite made an if-you-say-so face.

"You had to be there," Jodie said as she started unpacking the bags. "Sam seems to spend a lot of time with his nephews."

Margarite glanced over at her. "He should. He's their guardian. Their parents were killed in a hit-and-run accident about a year and half ago. I thought you knew."

The can Jodie had just pulled from the bag almost slipped from her hand. "No."

"Yes. Sad thing." Margarite placed the candied fruit next to her other baking supplies.

"So Sam's raising his nephews? Alone?"

"Yeah."

Jodie carried the canned goods to the pantry as she calculated. A year and a half ago…a couple months before her dad had filed suit. Talk about a double whammy—losing his brother and then getting sued for malpractice. With instant parenthood added in, he'd actually experienced a triple whammy. No wonder he hated her father. Joe had sued him at one of the most vulnerable times of his life.

"He seems to be taking his job seriously," she said when she came out of the pantry.

"Sam goes the extra mile." Margarite opened the fridge and started putting fresh vegetables into the drawers. "I remember when my sister's dog got hit by a car not long after he and his brother started the practice—"

"His brother was a vet, too?"

"They graduated a year apart. His brother did small animals, Sam did large. Anyway, Dave—his brother—wasn't at the clinic when my sister brought her dog in, its leg rolled out flat like a pancake. One bloody mess."

Jodie felt an instant surge of queasiness.

"You okay?" Margarite asked, giving her a sharp glance. Jodie nodded, doing her best to appear interested and not nauseous at the mental image she'd conjured up. "So anyway, instead of amputating, Sam worked for hours putting that leg back together. The bones, the muscles. Too many stitches to count. And he charged her only a hundred dollars, since she's on a limited income. She paid him ten bucks a month. He did the checkups for free."

"And the dog survived?"

"He's still alive. The leg's not one hundred percent, but he has it and can use it some."

No wonder Margarite thought Sam was a good vet.

"Did the accident take place here? His brother, I mean, not the dog."

"Vegas," Margarite said. "The Strip."

In Jodie's territory. "Did they catch the driver?"

"Oh, yeah." Margarite nodded with satisfaction. "They got him a day later. A casino executive, no less." Jodie felt an odd prickling sensation at the back of her neck. "He had prior DUIs," Margarite continued, "but had gotten off because he had the bucks to buy a good lawyer who cared more about money than doing what's right." She spoke with an edge of bitterness, then seemed to remember who she was talking to. "No offense."

"None taken," Jodie said faintly as she wadded up the empty plastic bags and stuffed them in the recycling box. She did not like the déjà vu nature of Margarite's story. Not one bit.

Don't be stupid. What were the chances...?

Casino exec...vehicular homicide while under the influence... Actually, the odds weren't that bad....

"You can probably see why you and Sam haven't exactly hit it off. Between your dad's suit and what happened to his brother, well, he's not real fond of lawyers."

"Do you happen to remember the name of the guy that killed Sam's brother and his wife?"

"No." Margarite eyed Jodie shrewdly. "Does the case sound familiar?"

"I might have read about it." She hoped that was all she'd done.

"I guess the news changes up pretty rapidly in Las Vegas, but here…it was all we talked about for a long time."

"I can imagine."

She needed to get a grip. There were tons of DUIs in Las Vegas. So many that some law firms specialized in them. Hers didn't. Her firm specialized in high-end clientele…such as casino CEOs. People who paid big bucks to have the consequences of their poor decision making tidied up as much as possible. She'd gotten DUI charges against "important people" dropped more times than she could count, due to police procedural errors, questionable Breathalyzer readings, whatever she could find to get a toehold and clear her client—one of whom was now serving time for vehicular manslaughter while under the influence. She hadn't defended him on that charge; he'd gone to another firm. But she had gotten him off for a prior DUI—the third strike that would have put him in prison.

"Losing Dave was hard on Sam, both personally and professionally," Margarite mused. "He really needs to get another partner, but I don't know if he's ready, you know?"

"Yeah." Jodie did not want to discuss Sam's business.

She wanted to get to a computer. Fortunately, the oven timer rang a few minutes later and she was able to make her escape while Margarite checked the roast.

Jodie booted up her Netbook in the privacy of her bedroom and went online. Less than three minutes later her hands fell away from the keys as she stared at the screen. Colin Craig, her former client, had been convicted of vehicular homicide in the deaths of David and Maya Hyatt.

Damn. So much for the pleasant edge of attraction. Or testing that shyness hypothesis.

Jodie turned off the computer and stood, gathering her thoughts, reestablishing focus and objectivity.

This was...unfortunate. Regrettable. Not her fault.

The cops had screwed up. Craig had hired her firm to prove that, and the case had been handed to her. She'd nailed the cops and earned a healthy chunk of change for the firm. It was all a matter of business. But now that she knew Sam and saw firsthand the aftermath of her successful defense, she had to admit it didn't feel that simple.

She pushed the thought out of her mind. Her dad would be the first to remind her that business was business...as sad as the outcome had been in this case.

So what now?

What now? She needed Sam. Theirs was a professional relationship.

He would never have to know.

CHAPTER SIX

"JODIE'S ALL RIGHT," Tyler said a little too casually as they walked into the house later that night after a fairly decent uncle-nephew outing.

Sam didn't reply. He would have to be dense not to see where this was going—where it had been going since his nephews invited Jodie to join them for dinner. The boys were trying to set him up.

Why?

And why Jodie? He couldn't think of a less likely prospect, considering the bad blood between him and her father. Surely one game of two-on-two hadn't impressed them that much. Although he had to admit to being a bit impressed himself. No. Make that a lot impressed. He liked this new side of Jodie. But...he looked at his nephews, who in turn appeared shifty...he was going to avoid complicating his life for a while. He didn't need to be distracted from his mission of raising his little brother's kids just yet.

"Don't you think?" Tyler persisted.

Sam picked up a sweatshirt that was draped over the back of a kitchen chair and handed it to him. "I think she's a good ball player," he said flatly. "Who forgot to load the dishwasher this afternoon?"

Beau let out a breath, raised his hand.

"Get on it. Then hit the books. If you have any questions, I want them ready for Miss Simms tomorrow morning."

"Yeah." Beau sounded way less than enthused, but he had to pass the next test in order to be able to play again. They only had a couple games before the zone semifinals and then possibly the state tourney. Without Beau, there was a question as to whether the team would qualify. He needed to be eligible.

Sam spent some time with Beau and his math, Tyler and English, and then he went to bed. But still he thought about Jodie. Yeah, he was attracted, which surprised him. And perplexed him. She'd had some challenges on the ranch, more than her fair share, but she was a strong woman. She shouldn't have that weird air of desperation every time something cropped up. Again he wondered how much Joe was to blame for that, and if Jodie was even aware of what she was doing, how she was reacting. Somehow he didn't think so.

JOE E-MAILED EVERY COUPLE of days for a ranch report and Jodie had just received her latest missive. Time to spin a heart-attack-preventing yarn.

It's still snowing on and off, but there's been no problem getting the animals fed. There've been some small challenges due to the snow, but nothing out of the ordinary. Lucas had told her that injuries and illness were a normal part of ranch life, after all. I'll fill you in when you get home, but so far nothing has happened I haven't been able to handle <g>. She had no idea if her father even knew what <g> meant, and it wasn't something she normally put in her messages, but what the heck? It gave the e-mail the no-worries feel she was aiming for.

So was she lying?

Damned right she was. It might be by omission, but she was shielding her father from the truth. Her one concern was hitting him with too much when he came back. However, if the bull recovered and the heifers calved safely, and the only incidents she had to fess up to were the cut horse and Mike quitting, then her dad would probably be ticked about being kept in the dark, and pout for a while, but it shouldn't raise his blood pressure.

She stared at her message for a moment. If she didn't add some specifics, then Joe would start asking direct questions. She put her fingers back on the keys. We had some trouble with the plumbing in the house. A pipe froze two days ago and the plumber came. We had to wait forever for him to arrive and it was a bitch not having water, but he thawed the pipes and reinsulated. He assured us it won't happen again. Also, the laser printer died, so I bought a new wireless model, which UPS delivered today. Hopefully I can get it up and running before you get home. She debated about another <g>, then decided against it. No sense pushing things.

There. She'd added enough reality that Joe wouldn't think she was sugarcoating. Jodie pushed Send and slumped back in her chair.

She was doing the right thing. She hoped. Joe should

be enjoying his vacation, not pacing the floor over what was going on at the ranch in his absence, driving his blood pressure up and her mother crazy.

So, when he came back, would she tell him about Colin Craig and Dave Hyatt while she was confessing the other truths? She usually told her father everything, but this…this she might just keep to herself.

SAM NEVER EXPECTED to relive high school, but that was exactly what he was doing. In the evenings, unless he had a call, he and Beau went over that day's math lesson, with books and papers spread across the antique oak kitchen table that had once belonged to his grandmother. Sam was brushing up on long forgotten skills. Beau had asked why he needed to learn math that hadn't been important enough for Sam to keep in his brain over the years. Sam had scrambled for a reply and finally settled on the benefits of building a base of knowledge, because you never knew what you might need to know. Plus the self-discipline was good for the brain. The answer sounded pretty decent, if he did say so himself. Beau was not impressed, but he had gone back to work on the problem that had him temporarily stymied.

Tyler went out Friday night without his brother, since Beau was grounded. He wasn't happy, but he didn't argue with Sam. Instead he sullenly continued to wipe down the kitchen counters while Sam put dishes into the cupboard.

"But I get to go tomorrow, right?" The basketball team was working at a local charity function.

"Yes, but you're not going out afterward. If Ty goes, you're coming home with me."

Beau looked as if he wanted to say something more, but just rinsed the sponge and headed for the kitchen table.

Four hours later the Beast pulled up to the house. Beau was sitting on the sofa, staring sightlessly at the TV, and Sam was almost asleep in his chair.

"Have a good time?" Sam asked with a yawn.

"Not bad," Tyler replied.

"What'd you do?" he asked casually, although he was also checking for the telltale odor of smoke or alcohol.

"Hung out at the bowling alley, which is why I smell like smoke," he said gruffly. "Then we went to the café for food." Tyler did not seem thrilled to give a recitation of his evening's activities—even an abridged one. He walked away without another word, shrugging out of his hooded sweatshirt as he headed down the hall to the bathroom. Sam watched him go, then shook his head and went to shut off the kitchen light before going to bed. It was his job to know what his nephews were doing, his job to see that they didn't get into trouble, which was so easy to do nowadays.

A few minutes later, he heard the boys talking in the bedroom they shared. Tyler was giving an expanded version of the evening, no doubt. Sam just hoped Beau wasn't hearing something that he himself should be aware of.

He took off his shirt and tossed it in the laundry basket in the corner of the room. Then he sat on the bed, resting his forearms on his thighs, his head bowed.

Dave and Maya should be the ones raising their boys, feeling the swell of pride when their sons did well, and propping them up when they didn't. Setting the rules, enforcing the consequences. Sam felt more at ease in his role now than he had a year ago, but he still saw the potential for disaster every time Beau and Tyler went out the door.

And he missed his brother. Sometimes he wondered how life would have turned out if he hadn't talked Dave into taking his place at the fateful veterinary conference, hadn't convinced him that Maya could use a little time away from Wesley. Would he have been hit by the car instead of his brother? Would Dave and Maya be mourning him?

Logically, it would have been better that way. Then his brother would have had the opportunity to see his boys grow into men, and Sam's nephews would have had parents who knew what they were doing.

Instead, Sam had the boys, the boys had him. All he could do was to hold on tightly and hope for the best.

IT SNOWED THE NEXT DAY, just as Lucas had predicted. Big lazy flakes drifted to the ground early in the morning, becoming a total whiteout by afternoon. Twenty-four hours later, the temperatures dropped and the wind picked up, piling drifts around the ranch buildings, to the point that any door facing north was unusable. The first calf dropped in the middle of the blizzard, but fortunately, the birth went well and Lucas had the baby and mama in the warm barn. If Jodie could have her way, all the animals would be in the barn. It was not weather for any creature to be out in.

For the most part the cows didn't seem to mind. They bunched together and put their butts to the wind, hunching up against the cold as their hair grew thick with rime ice. Lucas assured her that the animals had seen worse. They were all strong and well-fed, and the only ones he was worried about were the very pregnant heifers, which he had in pens near the barn, out of the wind and ready to be brought in if necessary. At least they were the only ones he worried about until the next morning, when the sun finally broke through, glinting off the crystallized snow. He went out to start the tractor to feed, and found part of the herd in the far pasture missing. At least five cows, maybe six. Each worth several thousand dollars.

"Where would they have gone?" Jodie asked when he came in to report. She already had a headache, having spent the morning trying to load the wireless printer she'd bought to replace the printer that had died the week before. Wireless had seemed like such a good idea at the time, but right now…

"That's what I need to find out," he said grimly. "The snow's so deep they probably walked over the fences."

"Won't they come home when they get hungry?"

"They should be hungry now and they aren't home. And I have two heifers ready to pop."

Jodie tensed slightly as she realized what came next, but all she said was, "I'll call Sam about the heifers."

This was what she was paying the retainer for. It was also an opportunity to make that first contact since learning she'd been inadvertently involved in his brother's death, to hammer home the point that her professional life was separate from her private life. It was indeed a sad situation, but the hard truth was she would defend Colin Craig the same way today as she had then. She was a lawyer. That was what she did.

So why did she keep having to repeat that bit of information to herself?

Because she'd never had a case that had crossed over into her personal life before. This was new territory. Territory she needed to conquer.

"Let me call," Lucas said. "I can give him the particulars." He went to the phone, and for once Margarite didn't grumble about slush on the floor, but simply headed to the cleaning closet for the mop.

Jodie listened as Lucas talked to Sam. Missing cattle. Oh, yeah. That would go over well. Her head snapped up when she heard Lucas say, "They haven't come back, so I'm afraid they may be in one of the culverts. Yeah, if the boys could come, that would be a big help. And Sam...I think the one heifer is carrying twins." He blew out a disgusted breath. "Yeah. Hope the county road is open. I plowed to the mailbox last night when the snow slowed down. There's probably only six inches or so on the road, but it may have drifted some. Okay. See ya."

"You think the cows might be in a culvert?" Jodie asked when Lucas hung up.

"Oh, no," Margarite said as she came into the room, mop in hand.

Jodie glanced from the cowboy to the housekeeper, not quite understanding. "How *big* are these culverts?"

"Big enough to handle flood runoff during wet years," Lucas said.

"Cattle walk through them to go from pasture to pasture," Margarite added. "And sometimes they take shelter in them."

"Wouldn't that keep the cows out of the weather?" Jodie asked, not understanding the problem.

"If the culvert drifts shut, the cattle can die of carbon dioxide poisoning." Lucas looked past Jodie to the housekeeper. He spoke to her when he said, "I'm going to saddle some horses, then head out. I'll check the culvert on the Gypsum Creek side. Margie, have the boys check the one on Samuels Creek. Jodie, you better go watch that heifer."

"What do I do besides watch her?"

"Just watch her. Sam will be here soon. I hope."

If the county road was passable.

"Why is my father in this business?" Jodie asked with a moan after Lucas disappeared back outside.

Margarite shrugged. "Keeps a body busy. And your father is fortunate that something like this won't make or break him. On a normal ranch, losing this many cattle would devastate them."

Jodie's insides went tight. "Don't talk about losing cows. I don't want my dad to have a heart attack when he comes home." And she meant that literally.

JODIE WAS IN THE BARN watching a confused heifer lie down and then stand up, over and over, when Sam arrived.

"Thanks for coming," she said when he walked into the barn.

"No problem." He set his equipment down and Jodie backed away from the paneled corral as if to give him room to work, putting her gloved hands deep into her coat pockets.

Sam seemed to be in no hurry to do anything. He walked from one heifer pen to the other, then stood back and watched the two animals deal with impending birth in their own way. In turn, Jodie studied the strong angles of his profile, wondering what it had been like for him to be plunged headlong into single fatherhood.

It couldn't have been easy….

"Are Beau and Tyler here?" she asked casually.

"They're already on their way to Samuels Creek."

"It's weird to think of them riding. They seem like such jocks."

"Lots of kids around here cowboy and play sports. My dad had a little ranch before he and my mom moved to the coast. The boys rode right up until he sold the ranch."

"Why'd your parents move?"

"My mom has asthma and couldn't take the desert allergens anymore."

"Oh." His mother had also lost a son.

Sam didn't get into the pen, but instead just watched the heifer, as Jodie had been doing. The only difference was that he probably had an idea of what to do if something did go wrong. He walked over to the pen where the second heifer stood breathing heavily, but other than that gave no sign that she was in labor.

And then the cow started to strain.

"She's standing up." Jodie stated the obvious, glancing at Sam and wondering what he was going to do about it.

"Some give birth that way."

"I see." Jodie swallowed. After all the hoopla about early calves and hard times for heifers, well, she just didn't know if she was ready to watch. So she didn't. She wandered over to visit Bronson in his stall. He hung his nose over the half door and Jodie stroked it. She heard Sam climb the panels and hoped it was for some routine reason.

"Jodie, I'm going to need some help here."

"Does it involve blood?" she asked. She was already on the move, willing to do her part, even if she threw up, but she wanted to steel herself.

"No."

"Be right there."

There was a tiny reddish calf lying in the straw, and Sam was peeling away the sac surrounding it. The cow was still standing, facing in the other direction. Sam handed Jodie a towel. "Rub," he said.

She took the towel and started gently rubbing it over the calf's long damp hair. The little guy was all bones and sharp edges. His head lay on the straw and his pink tongue was hanging out.

"No. Like this." Sam put his warm, weather-roughened hands over hers and began to briskly massage the calf. Jodie didn't know about the calf's circulation, but hers took an upswing. He smelled so damned good, and feeling his chest against her back…it was unfair that she had these reactions.

"This doesn't hurt him?"

"Gets her blood flowing and helps warm her."

Her. Okay. Jodie tried to keep up the movements as he went back to the cow, who was once again straining.

"Twins?" she asked.

"Yeah," he grunted. She didn't want to think about where his hands were right now. "But I don't believe this one is alive."

"Oh." Jodie rubbed harder and the calf's head started jerking around.

She kept her back turned as Sam continued to work. The calf started to wiggle more as Jodie rubbed it, trying to ignore what was going on behind her.

Finally she heard the sound of something hitting the ground.

"Is it alive?"

"No."

Jodie chanced a look over her shoulder, saw the cord hanging from the cow and instantly turned back to the calf. "Daisy," she said in an effort to distract herself. "We'll call you Daisy."

Sam continued to do whatever it was he did. She heard the sounds of something being dragged under the panel rails, and knew it was the stillborn animal.

She continued to rub until the calf made an effort to get her feet under her, and the mama cow started moving behind them.

"Better get out of the way," Sam said. Jodie stood up and, still clutching the towel with both hands, stepped back from the little reddish-orange baby. Sam climbed out of the pen and she followed. He reached for her, taking her forearms and helping her down.

The cow lowered her nose and sniffed at the calf now that she had the pen to herself. She sniffed again and then licked.

"Are we done here?" Jodie asked, glancing over at the other pen, where the cow was still going through the same routine as before. Up. Down. Up.

"I might have to tube the calf just in case it's too weak to nurse."

"Tube?"

"You probably don't want to know."

"Probably not," Jodie agreed. "What will you do with the twin?"

The stillborn calf was lying in the straw several yards away from the pen.

"Lucas will take care of it when he gets back."

"You see a lot of death in this job, don't you?"

He looked down at her, an unreadable expression in his gray eyes. "I see a lot of life, too."

The mother cow was licking enthusiastically now and the calf responded, first bobbing its head and then trying to struggle to its feet.

Sam and Jodie stood with their hands on the rails of the pen, so close that she could feel the warmth of his body, the solid muscles of his arm and shoulder against hers. She felt like leaning nearer, but couldn't.

"I may not have to tube, after all," he said.

As they watched, the baby managed to make it up to her feet, her tiny hooves wobbling on the straw-covered floor. The mama started nudging her toward the food source. The newborn stumbled, but managed to get her legs back under herself and totter a few steps toward the udder.

"Time for me to go to work." Sam turned his attention to the other cow. Sure enough, tiny hooves were showing.

"Please be alive," Jodie murmured.

"This is a normal presentation," Sam said as he climbed into the pen. "It's probably fine." He was right. Five minutes later a calf was on the ground, obviously alive and well. Sam climbed back out of the pen and let the mama figure out what to do next.

The barn door opened and they both turned to see Margarite hovering in the doorway.

"The boys just called. They found the cattle."

"Alive?" Jodie asked.

"Yeah. The culvert drifted shut only on one side. The herd couldn't get back through to the pasture. Lucas is on his way over with the tractor to help dig it out and move the cows back. Any calves yet?"

"Two," Jodie said.

"That'll make your dad happy," Margarite said. "I have hot drinks ready whenever you're done here." She shut the door, leaving Sam and Jodie alone once more. Jodie picked up the gloves she'd dropped before giving Daisy her rubdown.

"You do a lot to keep your dad happy, don't you?" Sam asked quietly as he began to pack up his equipment.

She slowly turned to look at him. "I'm trying to run this ranch to the best of my ability while he's gone, if that's what you're getting at." But she didn't think it was.

"What happens if you don't? What happens if you make a mistake? You know...leave a gate open. Injure a horse."

Jodie slapped the gloves on her thigh to remove the bits of straw and dust clinging to the leather. "He's going to be angry. He'll get over it." Eventually. After he'd had time to stew, then cool down.

Sam just shook his head and continued packing his equipment.

"Don't judge me or my family, Sam."

Jodie shoved the gloves into her coat pockets. She'd told her father the ranch would be fine in her care, and she fully intended to live up to that promise. Nothing wrong with that. So why was Sam questioning her?

"What's the deal, Sam? Why are you asking about my dad?"

His eyes were serious when he said, "I saw a different side of you when we played basketball."

"Yeah?" And what did that have to do with her dad?

"Yeah. You're nothing like you first came off."

She twisted her lips into a half smile, half smirk. She was slightly shocked at what he'd just said, but wasn't about to show it. "How did I first come off?"

He smiled slightly. "As someone who sees herself a step above the rubes who live here."

Her eyebrows rose. "You don't have to flatter me."

"I can't help myself," Sam said. "I'm a charmer through and through."

"I'm not a rube hater."

"No." He spoke gently, which somehow put her back up even more. "But what really bugs me is that you seem almost afraid to have your father come home to reality. This is a ranch, Jodie. Things happen. Emergencies are a way of life and, yeah, we try to avert them, but Joe's in this business. He knows what happens. Or he should. But you're desperately trying to hold things together."

This was pissing her off.

Leave it.

She couldn't. "Do you want to know how I first saw *you?*"

"No."

"I thought you were good-looking," she continued matter-of-factly. "And steady. You know…someone a person could depend on." His expression didn't change, but she had a feeling she was disconcerting him. Good.

"I thought you saw me as the incompetent vet who killed an expensive horse."

"That, too," she agreed.

"How about now?" he asked. "Right now?" He echoed her own words.

"I paid you a retainer, didn't I?"

"But you've never told me you thought I was competent," he pointed out.

Jodie smiled blandly. She'd had enough of this conversation. "Well, if you have everything under control here, I have to go wrestle a printer into submission."

She walked to the door, pushed it open and stepped out into the overly bright sunlight, pulling her coat around her as the cold air hit her.

Why was she so ticked off? It didn't matter what Sam Hyatt thought of her. In fact, it might be best if he did think poorly of her.

CHAPTER SEVEN

"I TRIED," Margarite said as Jodie walked into the kitchen, "but I couldn't get the darned thing to work."

"I'll see what I can do." Jodie left the kitchen and headed down the short hallway to the office, ready to do battle. She needed hard copies of accounts and Margarite wanted recipes. Both required a printer and somehow Jodie was going to get the damned thing hooked up.

She removed the installation disk, reinserted it and started loading. Again. And once again, after ten minutes of screens flashing on and off and green bars filling to show progress, the damned thing stalled out at 96% installation.

"*Damn* it!" Between printers, cows and vets... Jodie was about to fling the manual on the floor when she heard a noise in the doorway and looked up to see one of Sam's nephews—Beau, maybe?—staring at her. Color rose in her cheeks. Bartons didn't get caught throwing tantrums.

"Problem?" he asked matter-of-factly.

His expression was so earnest that Jodie squelched the impulse to snap, "No!" Instead she studied the boy's handsome face for a few seconds, wondering briefly if he looked like his dad, before she chased the thought out of her mind. “You could say that,” she said in a defeated tone. “I can’t get this printer to load and the other one’s shot. I need it so I can finish some work.”

“You want me to take a look?”

He was already halfway across the room and she had a feeling it didn’t matter if she said yes or no.

She nodded and stepped back. “I would love it.”

“Oh, yeah,” Beau said after taking a quick look. “If the initial installation doesn’t load on an Alto printer, then you’re screwed.”

“Great,” Jodie said flatly. “I’m screwed.” She didn’t mind buying another printer, but she didn’t want to wait the usual weeks for delivery out in the boonies, or to drive to Elko and pick one up, only to find that the new printer did the exact same thing.

“Not totally screwed,” Beau said, tapping the keys. “I’ll see what I can do. The problem is that you have this uncompleted command messing things up….” His voice trailed off as his fingers moved over the keyboard, his eyes glued to the screen.

“This is a nice computer,” he finally said. “You must have satellite Internet out here.”

“Yes.”

“It took us a long time to get Sam up to speed with his computer system. He fought us—” he smiled at the screen reminiscently “—but we eventually wore him down.”

This kid was cute. Intense and yet somehow sweet.

And standing behind him, watching him work, Jodie felt a whisper of guilt. She instantly tamped it down. What had happened was regretful. End of story.

"You want me to install these updates when I'm done?"

"Uh, yeah. Sure."

"Okay." He stopped typing and shrugged out of the heavy coat he wore.

"Where's your brother?"

"Waiting for me to come back to the barn. I came in to use the john."

"Do you think you should—"

"He's fine," Beau assured her. "Lucas had some stuff he needed help with while we're here. Grain to move and stuff. Sam's there, too."

Beau leaned closer to the screen to read a pop-up menu. He was so unconcerned about what he was supposed to be doing, while he rescued her.... Had to love him for that.

And again she felt a twist of guilt.

She had not orphaned this kid. *Get a grip!*

"Got it!" Beau sat back and stared proudly at the printer, which was now spitting out a test page.

"Thank you."

"Let me take care of this other stuff...." There was a commotion in the kitchen, male voices and stamping of feet on the mat as Margarite insisted that all snow and mud stay outside.

"Busted," Beau said when Tyler stuck his head in the office.

"Where the he...heck have you been?"

"Jodie needed help with her printer."

"Thanks for letting me know," Tyler grumbled, disappearing again. Beau stood up, looking satisfied.

"I think Margarite is going to feed you," Jodie said.

"Good. I hate cooking and it's my turn today."

"You guys take turns?"

"Sam says it's fair, since none of us like doing it too much." Beau picked up his heavy canvas coat and headed for the smell of roast beef fresh out of the oven. "Hey, if you ever need more computer help, just call me. I can probably talk you through stuff on the phone. Or I can until your dad comes home. Sam says we won't be out here any more then."

"I don't imagine you will," Jodie agreed. *Out of the mouths of babes...* "And thanks. I may take you up on that offer."

Everyone ate in the kitchen, leaning against the counters and talking. Or rather the boys were talking and Lucas was talking. Even Margarite tossed in the occasional comment. Sam and Jodie stayed at opposite ends of the kitchen, as far from each other as they could get.

"Hey, Jodie," Beau said at one point, "if you won't let us drive your car, can we ride in it? When the roads are clear?"

"And can we go fast?" Tyler added with mock eagerness.

"When *will* the roads be clear?" she asked, looking out the window to her left. "June?"

"Yeah, probably," Beau said. "But we can wait."

"I don't think I'll be here in June." Jodie gave a half smile. "But if you're ever down in my country, look me up."

Beau's expression instantly shuttered. "Yeah," he said. "Maybe."

Good one, Jo. His parents had died in her part of the country.

Margarite jumped into the conversation then, asking the boys whether the team would be going to the state tourney this year. The mood changed as Beau happily explained that he'd just passed a crucial math test and would soon be back on the team, so hell yes, they were going to state. Jodie stayed out of this conversation, choosing instead to listen and not make another faux pas.

Finally Sam brought his plate to the sink, next to where Jodie was standing. She ignored him as he set it in the basin of soapy water, and felt relieved when he told the boys that they had to get going. She needed some time to think things through, regain her perspective.

"Thanks for coming," Lucas said. "I appreciate the help finding the cattle and clearing the culvert."

"Hey, it was good exercise," Beau said with a grin.

"Glad we could help," Tyler added, and then the three of them went out the door. Both boys waved at Jodie when she stepped out to the glassed-in porch and watched them leave. All she got from Sam was his profile.

She folded her arms across her chest as the bronze

truck disappeared over the snowy hill. This situation with Sam and his brother was bugging the hell out of her, and that wasn't good.

If she lost her objectivity, then she might as well quit her job now.

"HAVE ANY CALVES BEEN born?" Joe demanded over the echoing computer-phone Skype connection. He'd had enough of e-mail and wanted to interrogate Jodie directly.

"Only two."

"What color?"

"A red one and a dusty brown." Lucas had told her the brown one would turn black, which was what her father was breeding the cows for. "The red one had a twin, but it was stillborn."

There was a slight pause, and then Joe said, "It happens. What sex are the calves?"

"Two girls."

Joe grunted with satisfaction. "Is Mike around? I'd like to talk to him."

"No," Jodie said with a clear conscience. "He's not available now." Nor would he be. "Everything is going fine." Nothing had died, except for the stillborn calf, and Bronson, the horse, was healing up better than Sam had hoped.

"Four more weeks," Joe said in a way that made Jodie think he was counting the days.

"Lu—" She almost said, "Lucas doesn't expect many early calves," but managed to change it to, "Lucky you, spending four more weeks in Europe."

"Yeah."

"Dad...aren't you getting anything out of this trip?"

There were a few seconds of silence and then he said, "I am enjoying spending time with your mother."

Jodie stilled at the unexpected response. That was perhaps the softest sentiment she'd ever heard her father express, and she needed to tread lightly so as not to ruin the moment.

"Well, you'll be back soon enough."

"Right."

"Keep in touch by e-mail, Dad. We agreed before you left."

"All right. Don't rat me out to your mom."

"I won't if you hang up now."

Jodie's shoulders sank with relief when he did as she asked. She hated lying, but right now the truth wasn't going to do Joe a diddly damn worth of good. She could see him hopping a plane home tomorrow if he knew that Mike was gone and she'd hired two people he never wanted on the ranch again to replace him. Tough. She was in charge at the moment. She'd fess up later, face-to-face. Hopefully that meeting wouldn't undo the good the vacation had done.

Although Jodie thought it was much too cold to turn a baby out, Lucas had let the new mothers and their calves back into the pasture. Daisy seemed to delight in the new freedom, galloping around her mama, peeking at Jodie from the safe side of the cow. And as Lucas had promised, she seemed oblivious to the cold even though there was a coating of ice on her long reddish-brown hair.

Jodie turned up her collar and went back to the house. She liked having Lucas there, liked not having to feed the animals in the below-zero temperatures. She'd already decided that come hell or high water, Joe was going to keep Lucas on. He'd been a bona fide godsend, as had Sam.

There was always the possibility, though, that Lucas wouldn't want to stay. Perhaps like Sam, he would refuse to work for Joe.

Jodie's gut told her he'd stay as long as Margarite was there. It hadn't been too difficult to figure out that Lucas had come back primarily because he was sweet on her and looking for a second chance after completing rehab. So far it seemed to be working. The housekeeper and the cowboy were spending more and more time together, and there was a lot less complaining about mud and slush on the floor. And that, Jodie decided, could be a trump card. Lose Lucas, lose Margarite. She didn't think Joe wanted to see his housekeeper go. The little woman might hate blood and snow, but she was more than capable of dealing with whatever emergency came up. Plus she was one heck of a cook.

"IT ISN'T LIKE WE'RE going to drink. We just want to go over to Chad's house for a while." Beau stood next to the kitchen door he and Tyler had been about to escape through when Sam had asked where they were going.

"His parents are in Salt Lake," Sam repeated for the third time. "You aren't going over there if his folks aren't home."

His nephews figured they were grown-up, now that they were driving, but Sam thought otherwise. They'd turned sixteen two months ago. That was not grown-up in his book.

Tyler's face was getting red with unexpressed anger. "There isn't going to be a party," he said. "You can come by and check. Even if there was a party, we don't drink."

Sam was exhausted after an eighteen-hour day, and this was the last thing he needed. But he didn't trust Chad Bellows and he didn't particularly like Chad's parents, either. They'd let their two boys run wild, and the older one had suffered some legal consequences because of it.

"Have Chad come over here."

Where were these well-worn parental phrases coming from? The exact same words that had driven him and Dave so crazy as kids were now spilling out of Sam's mouth.

"No!" Tyler said, the anger finally boiling over. "Either you trust us or you don't." Beau nodded, his expression taut.

"It's not you guys. It's Chad. His brother—"

"Made mistakes, but he's not there and he's not Chad."

That was it. Sam was too exhausted to argue any longer. "Stay home tonight," he said. Problem solved. He needed to crash and he didn't want to have to worry about the boys. And if they stayed home, maybe they'd learn not to question his decisions—which were made entirely for their own benefit. One of these days they'd understand that.

Sam shook his head as he walked down the hall to his room, leaving two angry teenagers staring after him.

He'd just pulled his boots off when the phone rang. A second later Beau called out sullenly, "You have an emergency."

Sam's chin dropped to his chest. If he could just get enough clients to pay up, he'd take on a partner. This was killing him. He went to the door in his stocking feet and opened it. Beau was standing at the end of the hall, his jacket still on, holding the cordless phone.

"Lawrences?" Sam asked. He'd sewn up a dog earlier that day, and Mrs. Lawrence had refused to let him put on a funnel collar to keep the animal from tearing at the stitches. If he had to go back and restitch that dog, he was charging double.

"Margarite."

His gut tightened for no particular reason as he walked down the hall. Beau handed him the phone, then slunk off through the kitchen to his own bedroom, radiating resentment.

Tough. Sam brought the receiver up to his ear. "Margarite?"

"They promised me if they both left there would be no problems," the woman said without a hello. No trouble figuring out who "they" were, since there were only two other people on the ranch.

"What's the problem?"

"What d'you think? I've got a heifer bred to a bull that was way too big, but the right color," Margarite said in disgust. "Can you come out here? Lucas had to go to Elko and Jodie's there, too, shopping. I can't pull this calf alone."

"I'll be right out," Sam said. He just hoped he didn't fall asleep driving to the ranch. He put the phone back in the charger, then called to the boys.

"Yeah?" Tyler replied from the living room, the TV now on.

"I'm going to the Barton ranch," Sam said wearily. He almost added, "Stay home while I'm gone," but stopped himself. The boys knew he wanted them at home that night. Hopefully, they'd do as he asked.

They'd *better* do as he asked.

JODIE'S PULSE RATE quickened when she returned home from a shopping trip in Elko—actually, an excuse to get out of the house now that the roads were plowed—and saw Sam's truck parked next to the barn. *Another emergency? A chance to see Sam?* It was ridiculous that the two thoughts held equal weight. She needed to figure a few things out here. Like why she couldn't get this guy out of her head?

She exited the ranch truck, which she'd driven in case it snowed again, and went straight to the barn. Sam was in a pen, tending to a new calf. He glanced up when the door opened, then pulled a long tube out of the calf's throat. The mother was still down.

"Yep, the incompetent vet is here, saving the day." Sam rolled up the tube as he spoke.

Jodie approached the pen and Sam looked at her through the rails. "Lucas said none of the heifers were ready."

"Cows are contrary creatures."

She eyed the tube, but didn't ask questions.

"Just a precaution," Sam said. He climbed the rails and dropped onto the other side, the tube and an empty bag in hand. "I've got to check this other cow."

Jodie started for the door. She had groceries to bring into the house, and since there was no emergency, she had no reason to hang around. She'd gone only a few feet when Sam let out a shout and the corral panels rattled. She whirled around, expecting to see him lying on the ground and the cow stomping him, but instead he had both hands pressed to his side, cursing and grimacing in pain. The cow was a few feet away, switching her tail, her eyes fixed on him in a belligerent bovine glare. Jodie had no idea what had just happened.

"Are you all right?" she asked, thinking even as she spoke that that was one stupid question. No, he wasn't all right.

"Ever heard of a cow kick?" he said through clenched teeth. "Get Lucas, okay? I need some help with this heifer."

"Get out of the pen, Sam. She doesn't look friendly."

The cow was eyeing him in a way that was not at all pleasant. Sam exhaled heavily, then, keeping one eye on the animal, whose tail swung back and forth rhythmically, he painfully climbed over the panels. Jodie automatically went to help him down off the rails, her hands dropping away from his solid back when he regained his footing and once again put pressure on his side.

Jodie's pulse was racing and she took a deep, steadying breath. Everything had happened so fast. She had never thought about how quickly the doctor could become the patient when a nasty cow was involved. The heifer snorted from her stall as if to emphasize the point.

"You're not going back in there," Jodie said.

Sam nodded in agreement, his hand still pressed firmly to his injury. "We'll put her in the squeeze chute."

"How badly did she get you? Let me see."

"I thought you didn't like blood." Her eyes flashed to his face. She must have looked like she was going to either pass out or render first aid, because Sam's expression changed. "No external bleeding," he said. "Just one hell of a hematoma."

"She didn't hit anything...vital."

He stared at Jodie for a moment, then a pained smile twisted his lips. "I think I'd know."

"I didn't mean... I meant an organ or something, not your..."

Sam met her eyes and the faint flicker of awareness between them was no longer so faint. Jodie felt a tumbling sensation deep inside. It had been *so* long since she'd found a man attractive—really attractive—and even longer since she'd slept with a guy.

"I'm fine," he said. "I just need Lucas to help me get this cow into the squeeze."

"Let me see what she did," Jodie insisted, "for legal reasons. I can't have you suing me later for injuries received on my property."

"That's your modus operandi, not mine." But he gamely lifted his jacket and pulled his shirttails up out of his overalls, exposing his side.

She swallowed hard when she saw the ugly purplish swelling where blood was gathering under the skin. "You need to get some ice on this." She swore the bruise was growing larger as she watched.

"It'll be all right." He spoke irritably.

"But—"

"I know a little about this stuff, okay?" He allowed the bunched up fabric in his hand to fall back over his exposed skin. "Besides, I can't go running for ice every time I get beat up a little. I'd have to install an ice-maker in my truck."

"Do you ever think about getting a new line of work?" Jodie muttered.

"Every now and then." His gaze connected with hers and once again Jodie felt a strong jolt. *Mercy.* "But you'd be in trouble if I'd done that."

"Deep trouble," she agreed, allowing her eyes to drift down to his lips, his very firm, gorgeously shaped lips, then back up to his eyes.

Oh, yes. He was feeling it, too, the strong sexual vibe between them. So…what to do about it? What was ethical? If he kept looking at her that way, what did she care? She leaned closer, could feel the warmth from his body. But when he put his free hand on her shoulder, he didn't pull her to him...he kept her from moving closer. Jodie instantly stepped backward, feeling an unexpected flash of embarrassment. Rejection sucked.

"Why?" she asked bluntly.

"Because it's not a good idea."

"Is it me?"

He said nothing. He didn't need to speak. She could read the answer in his expression.

"It is me." This was a first. She'd never encountered a guy who'd refused an invitation to explore an obviously mutual attraction—which made this doubly embarrassing. "How about a few specifics?"

"How about we just forget about this?"

She drew in a surprisingly shaky breath, which irritated her.

"Yeah. Maybe we'll do that." Jodie forced a humorless smile. "All right. Well...I'll just go find Lucas. Try not to bleed to death internally."

She started for the house. Part of her hoped he would call her back, that they could talk this through, but he didn't say a word and Jodie kept walking. She had her pride.

Which was about all she had right now.

Dollars to doughnuts four or five cows would have medical emergencies in the next couple of days and she'd have to swallow it and face him. Not that she couldn't do that quite well. It was just that...she didn't want to.

Sam Hyatt had done what no other casual acquaintance had ever managed to do. He'd hurt her feelings.

"Is SAM IN A MOOD?" Margarite asked as soon as Jodie set foot in the kitchen after finding Lucas and sending him to the barn.

"No...I mean...why do you ask?"

"You look peeved, like he snapped at you or something."

Jodie rolled her eyes as she turned to the cupboard for a teacup, irritated that her...peeved-ness...showed so clearly. Yeah, she was irritated. And embarrassed. After all, she'd just been shot down by a country vet. A really well-built country vet.

Now she'd probably never find out what he looked like naked.

Not that she should—it was just that it had been *so long* since she'd had sex.

She pulled a teabag out of the container on the counter and dropped it in the cup. *It's more than that.* Jodie closed her eyes and pressed her fingertips to her forehead as the thought struck her.

She also wanted to prove to herself that she didn't have to feel guilty about Dave Hyatt, and what better way to do that than to sleep with his brother? That was wrong on many levels, even if she was attracted to Sam.

"Vets and ranchers are notoriously surly during calving. Don't take it personally." Margarite brought the steaming teakettle over and poured water into Jodie's cup before refreshing her own.

"I'm not," she said, hoping that Margarite truly thought Sam had merely snapped at her. It would be too freaking embarrassing if she suspected the truth.

CHAPTER EIGHT

"YOU ALL RIGHT, SAM?" Katie came back into the office, where Sam had been staring into space.

"Yeah." Other than his side still hurting like a son of a bitch where the cow had nailed him, and not being able to get Jodie off his mind. He glanced at the folder Katie carried. "More bounced checks?"

"No. In fact, some of the checks I submitted paid this time. I called the bank and they reversed the fee on our account for Mrs. Newland's bad check, so I didn't have to charge it to her."

"Good," Sam said, trying not to sound distracted.

"Anyway, I just got a call from Stan Stewart. He's sick and can't make it for a scheduled C-section at the Flying W Ranch this afternoon. Would you mind filling in?"

It was a sixty-mile drive—past Otto, the small town to the south—but yeah, he was game. "Tell him I'll do it." The normally slow winter season had been unusually busy for Sam, thanks in part to Jodie, and was picking up even more now that calving was starting.

Sam pushed his chair back. "I'd better take off now,

so I can get back in time for math homework." Beau was off the bench and would play in the next game, but he had to keep his grades up.

Things had been strained for a couple of days after Sam had made them stay in that Saturday night instead of going to Chad Bellows' house, but the twins had started to come around after Monday practice. Sam was glad to have his boys back, but was more than aware that there would be new battles in the future as his nephews pushed the freedom envelope. Sam was all for them going out and having fun. He just didn't want them in a situation where they could make a mistake that would haunt them for years.

But was he being too strict?

"Hey, Katie..." She glanced up from her computer screen, her reddish ponytail brushing her shoulder. Sam hesitated. "Never mind," he finally said. He wasn't going to ask his twenty-year-old assistant if he was raising his nephews right. A perplexed look crossed her face, then she shrugged and went back to her work.

Things were going well. All Sam had to do was be vigilant for two more years.

THE GROCERY STORY PARKING lot was packed when Jodie pulled in on Friday afternoon, grocery list in hand. Suddenly, she seemed to be doing most of the weekly shopping, whereas before Margarite had done it all. Jodie didn't mind the chore, since it got her out of the house, but it made her wonder if Margarite and Lucas were taking advantage in a personal way of the time that she was gone. If so, she was happy for them... although it hardly seemed fair that Margarite and Lucas were getting some and she wasn't.

Not that she was going to try to travel that route with Sam again. Ever.

For the first time in her career, Jodie felt uneasy about her professional actions and entirely too responsible for a situation out of her control—which went against everything she'd been taught and had also led to one long, sleepless night.

She'd done her job and the judge had done his. Short of seeing the future, neither of them had had any way of knowing Colin Craig would ultimately kill someone. After all, she'd gotten more than one DUI charge dismissed with no repeat offenses.

Jodie put her head down to avoid the sleet as she crossed the parking lot. She could argue logic with herself all she wanted, but truthfully, the situation with Sam's brother bugged the hell out of her. So, of course, the first people she saw in the store were Beau and Tyler, each coming toward the exit with an overstuffed grocery bag.

"Hey," Beau said, his expression brightening.

"How's everything at the ranch?" Tyler asked as they stopped in front of her.

"Good," Jodie said, feeling as though she had I Helped Kill Your Parents stamped on her forehead. "No emergencies, anyway—I hope." She smiled.

"We kind of liked digging out the cows," Tyler said, shifting the groceries to his other arm.

"Oh, yeah. That must have been tons of fun," she said drily, thankful that she sounded normal.

Beau's face was the picture of youthful sincerity. "No. Honest. It was."

"Okay..." Why did these guys have to be so darned cute, like half-grown Great Dane puppies? "Are you playing yet?" she asked him.

"Yeah." He glanced down and then his gaze shot back up to hers as if he'd just come up with a brilliant idea. "You want to come to the game tomorrow?"

"Oh...I can't." The words popped out of her mouth almost before Beau had finished speaking.

"Why not?" he asked, taken aback by her instant refusal. "Big plans on the ranch?"

No. Being around you makes me feel guilty. And she hated the feeling.

"You want to go," Beau said, leaning closer in a conspiratorial way. "You know you do."

Tyler gave her a charming half smile. "We'd really like to have you there."

"Sure," she finally said, refusing to give in to the guilt.

"Good. We'll put your name down."

Jodie drew back. "Put my name down for what?"

"The family seats." Beau looked so earnest that the "whoa—wait a minute" died in Jodie's throat. The poor kid no longer had a family except for Sam, and grandparents too far away to attend the game. And no matter what part she'd played in that, she felt bad for him.

"Okay," Jodie said faintly. "Sign me up." It was only a few hours. And she really needed to clear this emotional hurdle, get her thinking back on track.

"Cool," Tyler said. "The junior varsity game starts at six. Ours starts at eight."

"I'll be there."

And damn it, she was going to enjoy the game. Jodie grabbed a cart and started cruising the aisles. Margarite was baking again, and if Jodie didn't spend as much time on the treadmill as she did, she'd be gaining weight. As it was, she was putting in an extra fifteen minutes morning and night, just to make certain her work clothes still fit when she got back to Vegas.

And how she wanted to get back to Vegas! With her own kind, where she wouldn't be seeing Sam every few days, and would once again have the Craig situation in perspective. She had friends there that would help her do just that. Gavin. Carmen. Friends who hadn't called her in a while, but hey, they were busy being professionals. And soon, she'd be doing the same.

"IS THAT WHAT YOU'RE wearing?" Tyler asked in a critical tone when Sam came into the kitchen late Saturday afternoon.

Sam glanced down at his jeans. They'd faded to pale blue, but hadn't sprouted any holes or anything.

"Yeah."

Tyler's lip curled in disgust. "It *is* family night."

"I wore jeans to family night last year." No one dressed for the event. It was simply a time when the players' parents or guardians sat in a special section of seats, and were acknowledged for support of the team with an announcement and bags of coupons and gifts from local merchants. They didn't go stand on the floor for everyone to see.

Something was going on. Sam could sense it. The silent communication between the twins, the fashion critique, the attempts to appear casual when both seemed to be feeling anticipation not tied to the game… Beau was excited to be playing again, but Sam couldn't shake the suspicion that something else was in the works.

The boys had to leave a good hour before Sam, giving them time to dress out, warm up. They had the Beast running when Beau popped back in the door. "You might want to get there a little early for good parking." Sam was aware of that and about to say so when Beau added, "And we invited Jodie to sit in the family seats."

With that startling announcement, he disappeared out the door, leaving Sam staring.

He'd been set up.

Sam wadded up the shirt he'd been taking to the laundry. *Shit.* Why had they invited Jodie? Had she cajoled them into it?

Unlikely.

She hadn't appreciated being turned down in the barn, although he doubted she was aware of just how difficult it'd been to walk away from her, figuratively and literally. His body had been thoroughly in favor of pursuing matters, despite his injury, but he had enough complications in his life without adding a sexual romp to the mix. However...maybe she had something to prove, to him or to herself.

All lingering suspicion that Jodie was in on the deal disappeared when he entered the gym and saw her sitting alone in the family seats behind the home team. She was dressed in jeans and a leather jacket, a green scarf draped carelessly around the neck, looking cool and regal, yet oddly uncomfortable at the same time. Out of her element. She was watching the warm-ups with too much intensity, as if trying to mentally remove herself from her surroundings.

Sam crossed in front of the stands, then went up the aisle and edged his way along the filled seats, saying hello about a half-dozen times before he sat down next to her. She glanced up, nodded a hello, but didn't say a word, which confirmed Sam's suspicion that she'd been set up, as well.

"How's it going?" he said lamely after a few seconds of uncomfortable silence.

"Fine." She turned her attention back to the warm-ups. The place was filling rapidly and the family seating was getting packed, bodies pressing together on the bench seats, yet Sam managed to maintain a few inches between himself and Jodie.

"The boys are glad you could come," he said.

"Hmm."

Okay, enough small talk. Jodie took rejection seriously. Which was what he had wanted. He just wished he didn't feel like a jerk for doing the right thing.

The pep band started playing and Sam focused on

his boys, who were shooting baskets. Every now and then one of them would glance over at him. He and the twins were going to have a talk tonight.

Beau and Tyler weren't the only ones interested in Sam and Jodie. He caught several people in midstare and a few pointing. He couldn't blame them for their curiosity. Everyone knew he despised Joe Barton, so what the heck was he doing here with Joe's daughter? In the family seats, no less.

If he was in their shoes, he'd be staring, too. For all intents and purposes, he and Jodie appeared to be a couple.

Sam let out a breath and glanced sideways. She continued to stare straight ahead, ignoring him. He had the urge to touch her arm, to draw her attention and tell her he didn't have anything to do with this, but instead he focused on his traitorous nephews down on the floor.

THE LONGER JODIE SPENT in Wesley, the more she became used to being scrutinized, and not in a good way. But tonight was worse than usual and it was getting to her. Had someone found out about her professional association with Colin Craig? Had Margarite put two and two together after their conversation in the kitchen the other day, and done some research of her own? Or were people simply perplexed because she was there with Sam, sitting in the family seats, where she had no business being?

It had to be the latter, since Margarite's attitude

toward her had not changed one iota. Jodie's connection with Craig was her own dark secret and she was again feeling guilty when she shouldn't.

Sam sat stiffly beside her, watching the activity on the court and taking care not to look at her. Oh, yeah, this was cool. She could smell the woodsy scent of the soap he used, which only heightened her awareness of him. Her nerves were humming with anticipation, though for what, she didn't know. It wouldn't be for a roll in the hay.

Maybe she should just tell him what she'd discovered. Get it over with.

No, because then she'd never, ever get a vet to the ranch.

Jodie forced herself to suck it up. Four quarters and she was outta here. Hopefully there wouldn't be many fouls or an overtime.

It turned out there were tons of fouls, and the game was not going well for the home team. The Warriors were down by fourteen points when the buzzer sounded at the end of the second quarter. Sam's cell phone went off at almost the exact same time. They'd been pushed together as more and more people crowded into the family seats, and were now sitting so close that she could feel the phone vibrate in his pocket. He dug it out and turned away, plugging an ear to try to hear over the noise in the gym.

After a few seconds of conversation, Sam snapped the phone shut and turned to Jodie, looking more than a little relieved. "I have an emergency. If I don't make it back, would you tell the boys I'm at Hartley's place?"

"Will do," Jodie said briskly. She couldn't say she was unhappy to see him go, but now she was going to be alone and the people who'd been wondering why she was with Sam in the first place could now wonder why he'd abandoned her. Well, screw 'em. She was there for Beau and Tyler. And for herself. Jodie propped her chin on her hand and watched the dance team perform, their sequined blue-and-red outfits sparkling under the lights.

When the performance was done, the announcer picked up the mic and proceeded to thank all those who made the games possible, those who contributed to the athletic program by volunteering or by making monetary donations. He especially wanted to thank the people who made the athletes what they were today, those individuals sitting in the family seats. Would they please stand and be recognized?

Stand? All Jodie had done was to have a few rather entertaining conversations with Beau and Tyler and play a game of two-on-two. But they'd invited her to the game, quite possibly to set her up with their uncle, so she stood with everyone else, feeling like a fraud.

Two more quarters, a quick thank-you to the boys, and she'd be gone. Hopefully before Sam got back. And in the meantime, she was damned well going to enjoy the game.

THE HARTLEY FAMILY lived fifteen miles from town, so Sam was at their place within a half hour of the call, ready to help pull a calf or do a C-section, depending on the situation. The Hartleys had only two cows and weren't exactly experienced, so Sam wasn't surprised to walk out to their small prefab barn and see a calf struggling to its feet.

"I take it you don't need me," he said.

Ned Hartley was petting the mother cow's face and beamed over at him. "I guess not. I thought the cow was all done in, and then out this little guy came."

Little was right. It was one of the smallest calves Sam had seen in a long time. The only way this would have been a difficult birth was if the calf had been coming out sideways.

"Sorry to interrupt, Doc." Ned left the cow and walked over to him, pulling a wallet out of his pocket.

"No problem. I'll be back before the game's over."

"How much do I owe you?" Ned flipped open the wallet and withdrew a tattered check. For some reason Sam wondered if it was his last one.

"I didn't do anything."

"Travel time?" Ned asked.

Sam waved a hand and headed to the truck. Ned didn't know it, but he'd done Sam a favor by calling.

The sounds of the excited crowd could be heard from the parking lot when he finally managed to wedge the truck into a very illegal space. He hoped all the local deputies were busy watching the game.

The noise grew louder and Sam quickened his step. Maybe the boys weren't getting trounced, after all. When he entered the gym, everyone seemed to be on their feet as Beau came thundering down the court, feinted left, then passed to his brother, who took the shot. In it went and all the players except for two raced to the opposite basket.

The score was 58-62 with two minutes left on the clock. Anything could happen in two minutes. A foul was called and the opposing center took his place at the edge of the key. Sam held his breath, then after the first ball bounced off the rim, he chanced a glance up to where he'd left Jodie. She was on her feet, her expression taut, her fists held together under her chin as she waited for the next shot. Another miss. Sam knew that only from the reaction of the crowd, since his eyes were still on Jodie. Play started again and her fists dropped to her sides as she leaned forward to yell encouragement to the team.

She could have left after he did, but she'd stayed to watch the game and now she was cheering for the team for all she was worth. And, Sam had to admit, she was beautiful while she did it.

The coach called a time-out and the crowd slowly sat back down. Sam made his way to his seat while he could, once again coming from the aisle closest to the door and edging through the crowd, since the home team was taking up all the space along the edge of the floor. Jodie glanced up at him as he approached, her face flushed with excitement.

"It's a good game," she said, turning her attention back to the floor.

The whistle blew and the clock started. The rest of the game passed in a blur, possession passing back and forth between the teams. Jodie grabbed Sam's shoulder when Beau made a basket, making the score 62-64, then realized what she was doing, and let go as if she'd just been burned.

"Come on, guys," she muttered. He could feel her body vibrating with excitement as the Warriors went into a press.

"Oh!" Jodie fisted her hands again when Tyler stole the ball from the opposing team and then passed off to Chad Bellows. Sam may have had reservations about Chad, but had to admit the kid was either talented or lucky when the three-point shot whooshed through the basket. The opposing team rebounded, racing down the court as the last seconds ticked away. A player shot from the center line just as the buzzer rang. Jodie gasped, then pressed her fists to her chest when the ball bounced off the rim. A second later she was jumping and cheering with the rest of the home team crowd at the comeback win.

Sam joined in the cheering, but his eyes were on Jodie.

She could have left. She didn't. He'd embarrassed her in the barn. Maybe he needed to make some amends here. Maybe they could at least be friends?

CHAPTER NINE

SAM MADE HIS MOVE before he could talk himself out of it. He leaned closer to Jodie so she could hear him over the crowd. "You want to go grab a bite somewhere?"

Her demeanor instantly shifted, as if she suddenly remembered where she was, who she was with. Her eyebrows lifted slightly as she said, "I think the good people of Wesley have had enough to gossip about tonight. They don't need more."

"Why not?"

"Because..." Her voice trailed off momentarily before she said firmly, "Because."

"And you call yourself a litigator?"

She flushed slightly. "Look, Sam. A few days ago you said we shouldn't pursue...things. I agree with you."

"Maybe I changed my mind."

She rolled her eyes heavenward. "Just like a man," she muttered before edging away from him and into the crowd of people moving down the stairs toward the gym floor.

Sam followed, putting a light hand on her upper arm so they didn't get separated. He leaned close again when they came to a stop as an elderly woman struggled out into the aisle ahead of them. "How's that?"

"Wanting what you can't have."

"I probably could have had it a few days ago…."

He felt Jodie's back stiffen slightly before she glanced over her shoulder at him, her blue eyes candid. "But you dithered. Too bad for you."

Sam grinned for real. "Come on. One drink. Start off on a new foot."

"Where will we be going on that new foot?"

He shrugged. "Who knows?"

"Shouldn't we wait for Beau and Tyler?" she asked as they stepped down onto the floor. He'd yet to let go of her arm, and people were indeed taking notice.

"It takes them awhile. We usually meet up at home. I'll give them a call on our way to the Supper Club."

They moved with the crowd toward the exit. Jodie walked silently beside him. "All right," she finally said. "One drink."

Sam called the twins' phone as he drove to the restaurant, following Jodie's Spitfire. She parked in the half-full lot and he pulled up beside her just as Tyler finally answered.

"I'm going to be at the Supper Club."

"You are?" Tyler said with mock surprise.

"Yes, and it isn't because you set us up. Jodie and I have some business to discuss."

"Oh, Jodie is going with you?" His nephew spoke with exaggerated innocence.

"Do not pursue a career in acting," Sam advised. "I want you guys home by eleven."

"No problem," Tyler said in his normal voice. "Have fun." He hung up before Sam could reply.

Jodie was waiting beside her car, her hands shoved deep into the pockets of her leather coat, her scarf wrapped so that it covered the lower part of her face. He pocketed the phone and got out of the truck. The wind was picking up and before long snow would be falling. He just hoped it held off until eleven, after the boys were home.

"Come on," he said, jerking his head toward the entrance. "It's cold out here."

"I'm originally from Chicago. This isn't cold."

They mounted the steps and Sam held open the large wooden door as she ducked in under his arm.

The club was busy with a happy after-game crowd, but there were still plenty of tables in the lounge area.

"Dinner tonight?" the waiter, a young guy in jeans and a Wrangler shirt, asked as he handed over drink menus.

Sam glanced at Jodie, who shook her head. "Drinks," Sam told him.

"Cool. What can I start you with?"

"Bud," Jodie said.

"The same."

"They're watch-ing us," Jodie said in a singsong voice, stating the obvious when the waiter left.

"Of course they are. Your dad tried to destroy me not too long after I'd lost my brother."

"That wasn't what he was trying to do." Jodie automatically defended him.

"Oh, I think that's exactly what he was trying to do, because that's how Joe tackles life. Kill or be killed."

"How do you know that?" Jodie asked softly. She seemed surprised by his perception—or maybe that he'd stated it aloud.

"Because I've spent some time with him?" Sam said, thinking that the answer was obvious. "Are you telling me he's not like that?"

"I guess what I'm telling you is that he felt justified in what he did. It wasn't that he singled you out for extraordinary retribution."

"Just regular retribution?"

Jodie bit her lip as she glanced down at the table. When she looked back up there was a glint of grudging amusement in her eyes, which faded when she said, "I think my father was surprised at the town's response to the lawsuit."

"He shouldn't have been." Unless he thought he was too important to suffer consequences for his choices. "People in isolated communities tend to hang together. It's the only way they could survive back in the day, when resources were difficult to come by. The spirit remains."

"Do you think they'll ever become more accepting?"

"They will tolerate him, but no, I don't think he'll be accepted. And I can't see that it would matter to him." Joe used the ranch as a showcase and a hobby. A place where he could pursue his urge to compete, and could fly people in for fancy getaways. During the summer he had a crew of four or five college kids who worked around the ranch and served as guides and general help when he had guests—which was just about every weekend. None of the kids were ever local. He did seem to hire ones who knew what they were doing, though.

"Other than when he needs vet work."

"Other than that. I'm surprised he didn't make arrangements with Eriksson to come up and live here during calving."

"He had Mike...or thought he had Mike."

"So how has your dad taken the news of Mike quitting?" Sam started shrugging out of his jacket.

"He doesn't exactly know."

Sam stopped with his arm halfway out of his sleeve. "You haven't told him?" Whether she admitted it or not, he still believed that Jodie was afraid of messing with her dad. He'd seen her go head-to-head with Joe in a lawyerly way at social functions; she wasn't afraid of debating with him, but it seemed she was deeply into censoring life at the ranch to keep Daddy happy.

"I haven't told him." Her classic cool expression slipped into place, but her fingers were busy lightly pleating the napkin in front of her.

Sam pulled his arm out of the other sleeve and dropped the heavy leather coat over the back of the chair. "He's probably going to find out. Why not tell him now?"

"He's taking a grand tour of southern Europe to keep my mother happy. Greece, Italy. But actually...the trip is more for his health than for my mom. I don't want to give him a reason to come home or to worry."

"What's wrong with him?" Sam asked, leaning his forearms on the table and watching Jodie as she spoke. It was all he could do not to ask what was wrong with *her,* why she seemed so different tonight. Almost evasive. It wasn't simply because his nephews had conned her into the family seats and tried to set them up. He'd bet his truck on it, and he couldn't afford to lose his truck.

"Some heart irregularities, and he's stubborn about changing his lifestyle and his stress level. My mom was hoping the trip would help him get a different perspective on life. He's been in competition with the world for almost sixty years. Mom wants him to see that maybe he can run the ranch as more of a relaxed hobby than a cutthroat business."

"Think it'll work?"

"No. But I'm hoping his blood pressure will be back under control when he returns."

"If he's got trouble with blood pressure, ranching may not be his best bet for retirement."

Jodie huffed out a breath. "Try telling him that." She smoothed out the napkin. "My dad is not a bad guy, Sam. He's kind of a larger than life person. He's accomplished a lot by demanding the best and accepting no excuses."

Sam just nodded and smiled. In other words, he was a bully.

JODIE WAS CONFUSED. Here she was, sitting in the Supper Club with Sam, who'd turned her down when she'd hit on him in the barn. Sam, who could have disappeared after his emergency call and she never would have known.

Sam, who'd insisted on a drink and was now watching her in an intense way that made her feel even more self-conscious than she'd felt at the game.

There was a brief lull in the conversation after she'd confessed Joe's health issues, so she broke it, wanting some answers. Now.

"Why'd you ask me out for drinks?"

Sam settled back in his seat, making the chair creak with the movement. "Why'd you come to the game?"

"The boys asked me. It seemed important to them."

His voice was low, his eyes steady on hers when he said, "That's why I asked you out."

She frowned, shaking her head slightly just as the waiter came back with two bottles of Bud and two glasses. He expertly poured the glasses half-full and set them beside the bottles. "Anything else?"

"Not just yet," Sam said with a touch of impatience, his eyes on Jodie.

"I'll check back with you."

"You asked me out because your nephews wanted you to?" Jodie continued once the waiter had moved off to another table.

"No," Sam said evenly. "It was because you were nice enough not to disappoint them."

"Surprised?" Jodie heard the edge in her voice. Her beer sat in front of her untouched, her hands folded neatly on the table, one on top of the other.

He shifted in his seat again and she found herself focusing first on his mouth and then the angles of his face. Had his brother been this good-looking? The twins resembled Sam, so he must have been.

Not your fault.

Then why does it feel like my fault?

"Maybe. You were pretty caught up in the game."

"I like basketball."

"What else do you like, Jodie?"

"I, uh, like my job." She loved her job. Or most parts of it.

He smiled slightly. "Good."

"Long walks in the rain."

"There's a lot of that in Las Vegas."

One corner of her mouth quirked in acknowledgment. He continued his steady appraisal and she thought of a few more things she liked. "I go to every Rebels game, basketball and football. I've started taking karate classes, but I'm not too good at it. Yet." Or maybe ever. She was really bad at karate, but wanted some kind of self-defense training. She was, after all, a single woman in a big city. She glanced down at her hands. Her nail polish was chipped. "It's been awhile since I've hit on a guy, Sam."

She had the satisfaction of seeing surprise cross his handsome features at her rapid change of subject. "Usually men hit on me. So, come to think of it, you might be the first guy I've hit on since my divorce." And he'd shut her down.

"How long ago was that?"

"Five years."

Sam looked shocked. "How old were you when you got married?"

"Twenty-two," Jodie said sheepishly. "I'm ashamed to say I don't even feel like I've been married for real.

It only lasted three years. We were very young and dumb and totally unsuited. He spent all his time at his restaurant and I spent all my time studying and then working." She smiled sadly. "We just grew apart. We tried counseling for a while, but Damian's heart wasn't in it. I think my dad was unhappier about the divorce than either of us."

"Your father approved of Damian?"

"He came from a wealthy family," she said with an ironic smile. And maybe she'd married Damian because her father had approved so heartily.

Sam looked at her in his direct way. "Why me, then?"

"I was curious."

He glanced down. "Sorry if I was less than tactful that day."

"No. You were tactful. To the point, but tactful. Which is why I'm surprised to be here tonight."

"Yeah. Well…my personal life hasn't been the same since I took guardianship of Beau and Ty."

Another small twist of the knife. "So it wasn't just me," she replied, attempting a light note.

"I want their lives as stable as possible while I have them. It isn't easy to wake up one morning to the news that you have no parents. My brother's family was tight."

Jodie hoped her face didn't go white. She lifted the glass she'd ignored up until now, and drank. "So you have the boys at home for, what? Two more years?" She felt as if she was curling up inside, and fought against it. Yes, she was very, very sorry Dave Hyatt had died. She was sorry she'd had to point out that the police had messed up. But that was her job and she'd done it.

"If they go to college, which I hope they will."

Jodie nodded, wondering if the tuition would be paid by a life insurance settlement.

"I want them to get their feet back under them before they head out into the world. Keeping them stable is important to me." Sam ran a finger over the condensation on his glass. "Maybe the *most* important thing to me."

The door opened and a whirl of snow came in with the small crowd of people.

"I guess the storm showed up." Sam reached for his phone. "I want to touch base with the guys. Do you mind?"

Jodie shook her head and he punched a number. She could hear the phone ringing from where she sat, then the muffled greeting of voice mail. Sam frowned and redialed. This time there was a pickup.

"Tyler...are you guys at home?" Sam listened for a few seconds and then said, "It's snowing. Maybe you'd better—" A chorus of raucous whoops came through the receiver so loudly that Jodie heard them. "Where are you?"

She glanced away. *Oh, boy.* When she looked back at Sam, his frown had deepened and his jaw was set in a way that reminded her of her dad.

"Go home," he demanded into the phone. "I'll meet you there in ten minutes.... Then you'd better *find* Beau and get your asses home. Now!"

Sam shut the phone, his mouth still so tight his lips were almost white. "I, uh, need to go."

"I understand," Jodie said, glad to escape, although she wasn't thrilled about the circumstances. Single parenthood wasn't easy and Sam had jumped in during the most challenging years of a kid's life.

He flipped a twenty on the table and stood. Several heads turned as he and Jodie headed toward the door. She kept her chin up, ignoring everyone, and followed him outside, where they were hit by a blast of wind.

It hadn't started snowing hard yet, but what little snow had fallen was blowing into small white cyclones and somehow shooting down Jodie's neck. She pulled the collar of her jacket tighter.

"Sorry you didn't get to finish your drink," Sam said when they got to her car, "but maybe it's best that you get the Spitfire home before the snow starts for real."

"Yeah," Jodie agreed. It was best. Why did she have such a hard time looking away from him?

Why couldn't their circumstances be more normal, so she could explore this...situation more thoroughly?

Sam seemed to be thinking along the same lines. He smiled slightly, then stepped forward and took her face in his chapped hands, tipped her lips up and kissed her.

Jodie didn't move at first, stunned as she was by the instant heat that surged through her. She forgot about wind and snow and cold necks as his warm mouth moved over hers. She let go of her coat and ran her hand up his leather jacket, her bare fingers gripping his shoulder.

"You're good at that," she murmured when he lifted his head. She was already missing the pressure of his lips and wanting very much to pull his mouth back to hers. Too bad she'd never find out what else he was good at.

"Call me when you get home," he said after leaning in to give her another quick kiss. "So I know you made it okay."

"No." She could still taste him.

His eyebrows went up.

"You aren't going to add me to your list of duties," she said.

"Please." The word came out roughly, as if he wasn't used to using it.

She pulled her keys from her pocket. "Sam, go home to your boys. You have a situation and you don't need to be distracted by me."

THE BEAST WAS IN ITS usual spot when Sam pulled into his driveway. He didn't know what had him feeling more unsettled—the way he'd just parted from Jodie or the prospect of dealing with the twins.

They were sitting at the kitchen table, obviously waiting for the interrogation, when he came in. Neither boy looked nervous; instead their expressions were annoyingly self-righteous, considering the circumstances.

"Have you been drinking?" Sam demanded. He and his brother had done their fair share of partying as kids, but he had a whole different perspective on the matter now. Parenting was not for the faint of heart.

"We're on the team," Beau said indignantly. "We don't drink."

"And after what happened to Mom and Dad," Tyler added in such a low tone that Sam could barely hear him, "we aren't going to drink and then drive the Beast home."

His nephews spoke with total honesty, but Sam still came closer, took a whiff. They smelled of smoke, not necessarily the legal kind, but there was no scent of either alcohol or breath mints.

"I can't believe you did this."

"We didn't do anything," Tyler snapped back angrily. "We stopped at the party. We fully intended to be back by curfew—which we are, and not because you called."

"How many other times have you done this?"

"What?"

"Gone to parties when I thought you were just out with your friends."

"A few," Beau admitted.

"We've never done anything wrong," Tyler reiterated.

"We have taken kids home, though," his twin admitted.

"You're the designated drivers?" Sam asked in surprise.

"The DDs? Sometimes." Neither boy looked repentant. "Sam, we're sixteen years old. We can make decent decisions."

"Sixteen is not exactly an age known for decent decision making. If you go to parties, it's easy to get into things you shouldn't."

"It's also easy if you don't go to parties. We've talked about this and made our decisions." Beau spoke with conviction.

"You have, have you?"

"Yeah." Beau glanced over at Tyler in that way that made Sam think they could actually read each other's thoughts. Ty nodded. "And we've talked about some other stuff, too."

"Like what?"

"Like we need *you* to get a life so that *we* can have a life."

"What?" Sam asked incredulously. "How did this get twisted around to me?"

"You need to relax and stop trying so hard," Beau said.

"Trying so hard."

"I mean we appreciate it and all, but it's not helping anything. It's like you're trying to make up for us losing Mom and Dad, and you can't do that. You just—" Tyler shrugged helplessly "—can't."

It was the first time the boys had so casually mentioned losing their parents, and they'd just done it twice in one conversation.

"I owe it to your dad to see that you're brought up right."

"And you're doing a good job, but...you kind of..." Tyler looked over at his twin. "What's the word?"

"Smother," Beau replied.

"Micromanage," Tyler corrected.

Sam's mind was reeling. If this was a ploy to sidetrack him from grounding them because of the party, it was working pretty damned well.

"If you just relax, you'll be less stressed, and we'll do our best not to become delinquents." Tyler glanced at his brother. "Well, I promise not to be a delinquent."

"Me, too," Beau agreed, in such a solemn tone that Sam felt like laughing. But then again, he didn't. What the hell?

He needed a drink, but there was no way he could pour one without setting a bad example for the boys.

"You're still grounded for going to the party without telling me."

"So if we tell you…?"

"No," Sam said adamantly, then rethought the wisdom of taking a tough stance right now. "We'll discuss it later." After he'd had time to think about it. "And—" he hesitated briefly "—we'll talk about other stuff, too."

Beau and Tyler exchanged glances, then Tyler cleared his throat and said, "We know that having us here has been kind of hard on you. That we've kind of made it so you can't…" Tyler's voice trailed off and Beau finished.

"Go out with women and stuff like that. Like you used to do. Before."

Sam's life *had* changed dramatically since the boys had moved in, but he hadn't realized they'd noticed.

"Is this why you set me up with Jodie?"

They nodded in unison.

"She's hot," Beau said. "And I like her. We kind of thought you liked her, too."

Sam pressed a hand against his forehead. "So you're saying I've been overprotective and..."

"Probably have blue balls," Beau said solemnly.

It seemed like a good time to end the conversation.

"We'll talk tomorrow," Sam said, feeling totally outmaneuvered. "Maybe not about the blue...whatever, but the other stuff."

"All right." The boys got out of their chairs and Tyler clapped Sam's shoulder in an empathetic gesture before silently leaving the kitchen and heading down the hall to the pit the boys called a bedroom. Beau hung back for a moment.

"Sorry about Jodie. I really did think you kind of liked her. And if you guys hit it off, then..."

"Problem solved for you and Ty?" Sam asked. Micromanaging uncle distracted—although he still didn't fully agree that that was what he'd been doing.

"And maybe for you, too."

"'Night, Beau." Sam wanted to end the conversation before his monklike lifestyle came back into play.

"'Night."

CHAPTER TEN

JODIE BEAT THE SNOW HOME for the most part. A couple of inches had accumulated by the time she turned onto the Zephyr Creek Ranch road, but the trip had been uneventful, except for the wind trying to blow the Spitfire into a ditch. It was good that she hadn't had to focus on her driving, since most of the way home she'd been replaying her evening with Sam and trying to figure out her next step. *Oh, that kiss.* She'd had a feeling that she and Sam would have some chemistry if they ever got their hands on one another, but she couldn't remember the last time she'd connected like that with a guy—quite possibly because she never had. Not even with Damian when they'd first hooked up. Was a long celibate streak to blame? She didn't think so. The sparks had felt genuine.

More's the pity.

She'd just pulled the Spitfire into the garage when her cell phone rang. Her pulse bumped up slightly when she realized it was Sam.

"Are you home all right?" he asked gruffly.

"I thought you weren't going to add me to your duties."

"Are you home?" he repeated.

"Yes," she said softly. "I just got here." *And I can't quit thinking about you.*

"Good."

There was a brief silence, then Jodie said, "Is there anything else?"

"Probably," he replied in a tone that made her pulse quicken. "I'll talk to you later."

He hung up before she could say goodbye. Jodie held the phone for a moment, staring down at it as if expecting it to tell her what to do. Then she flipped it shut and let herself out of the car.

It appeared that Sam wasn't going to just go away after that kiss, and now she needed to decide on a course of action.

FOR THE FIRST TIME in a long time, Sam was awake for a good part of the night and it had nothing to do with a veterinary emergency. Had he screwed up, the way he was raising the boys? Was he smothering them as Beau had suggested?

How much of their complaint was from the teenage need for freedom and how much was justified? He wished he knew. The boys were still recovering from the loss of their parents, but maybe Sam had been overcompensating, trying too hard to do what he thought Dave would do. Acting more from emotion than anything. He wanted to do the right thing, and he was desperately afraid of making a mistake.

He was also exhausted from second-guessing every decision he made. He missed his old life, but he had a commitment here.

Last night had been the first time they'd mentioned their parents' deaths in casual conversation. The boys had gone through grief counseling in Elko after David and Maya had died, but they'd been uncomfortable with the counselor and after three sessions had begged Sam not to make them go again. He hadn't been that comfortable himself and wasn't certain whether it was because of the counselor or part of the grief process. The boys had settled back into their lives well enough, though, and Sam thought he'd been doing a pretty good job of parenting—for an amateur—up until last night. But no matter how normal things appeared on the surface, they rarely talked about David and Maya.

Had he made a mistake there, too?

Monday morning, after the boys had gone to class, Sam called Tricia Lopez, the guidance counselor at the high school, from the vet clinic office. He'd winged it for too long. It was time for some advice, or at least another opinion.

Tricia was a Wesley native, but had only recently moved back to take the counseling position. Because of that, she asked Sam to explain the situation from the beginning—if he was comfortable sharing. Sam shared. He poured the story out, surprised at how much he had to say, then waited for the verdict. When Tricia didn't answer immediately, his stomach dropped. He *had* screwed up. "Are you still there?"

"Yes, I'm here." He could hear reassurance in her voice. "I was just jotting down some notes."

"So what do you think?"

"I think you're trying very hard to be a good parent,

but you need to be careful not to…set too high a standard for yourself because you feel you owe it to your brother to raise his children perfectly."

That was exactly what he'd been doing. The big question was how to stop. "All right," Sam said slowly, jotting down a few notes of his own.

"Most teens think their parents are micromanaging," Tricia continued. "There's a thin line between doing more than you should and not enough, and no matter what, kids are going to push the envelope. It's your job to push back. Just be aware of trying to control too much."

"Will do." Or at least he'd try. How was he supposed to know what was too much?

"And as for the other…the boys have a point. Shutting off your own life isn't helping matters. If you don't meet your own needs, then how are you going to meet theirs?"

"I was just thinking that in order to keep things stable, I should…I don't know."

"But I *know* you, Sam. You're always going to be there for those boys and you're going to make good decisions. Just having you around makes their life stable."

"Should I bring up David and Maya? Talk about them more?"

"I think that might be a good idea. You'll know if the twins are uncomfortable with it. Trust your instincts."

"Thanks."

"May I ask a favor?"

"Sure. What?" *Free inoculations? A neutering? Name it.*

"Do you remember Paige Mansfield?" Tricia asked. "She was a couple years behind us in school."

"Vaguely," Sam said, wondering where this was going.

"She lives in Elko now, but comes into town once a week to do specialized counseling—"

"We already tried grief counseling," Sam said. "It didn't go well. I'm no expert, but I think she made the boys talk about too much, too soon."

"Paige is a family counselor and she's really good at not pushing. If you're interested in trying just *one* session to see how it goes, she uses my office in the evening, after practice is over." Tricia paused, then said, "I can put you guys on the schedule for this week. Tomorrow. You could try one session…."

What did he have to lose? "Sign us up," Sam said, although his gut was clenching.

"You're going to love Paige," Tricia said with a note of satisfaction in her voice. "And I honestly think she can help you through the twists and turns of adolescent parenting."

"Damn, I hope so."

THE BOYS WERE UNUSUALLY quiet when they got back from practice Monday night, making Sam wonder if Tricia had called them in to talk to them. He hoped not, unless she honestly thought it was an emergency. He didn't know if they would appreciate him sharing with a stranger, even if she was one of his childhood buddies.

"Hey," Beau said as he actually took his dirty practice uniform to the laundry room instead of dumping it in a smelly wad on a kitchen chair.

"Hey," Sam echoed faintly. "How was practice?"

"Coach says if we play like we did on Saturday, we'll get to state for sure."

"I agree. That was a great team effort."

The three of them stood in awkward silence for a moment. Sam had gotten off work at five, so he'd cooked hamburgers, which were now ready to eat. But for once the boys didn't mention food.

"We really hope we didn't, you know..." Tyler shrugged and glanced at Beau, who for once came up with the words instead of the other way around.

"Hurt your feelings or anything last night."

"You surprised me. That's all."

"Sorry about the blue balls comment," Beau mumbled, in a way that made Sam think Tyler had discussed the matter with him.

"Okay, here's the deal," Sam said, cutting to the chase. "I'm new at this parent game and I'm damned afraid of making a mistake. And, uh, there's this family counselor who comes to town and we're going to go see her."

The boys exchanged horrified looks.

"No," Beau said adamantly. "Not that again."

"She's supposed to be different. Better."

Tyler said nothing. He didn't have to—his grimace said it all.

"This is moreso that I know when to cut you loose and when to lay down the law." Sam figured that the prospect of more freedom might appeal to his nephews. "And maybe she'll see some things we're missing. Like me not knowing that you guys felt smothered."

There were no raucous cheers of agreement.

"One session," Sam said, "and then we'll reevaluate."

The proposal was again met with stony silence.

"One."

"All right," Tyler finally agreed. "But she better not be like the last counselor." Beau gave a slow nod, looking none too happy.

"We'll find out pretty soon. We're going to see her tomorrow night after practice."

"Whoopee," Tyler muttered under his breath.

Sam didn't want to admit it, but he felt the same. But he was adamant about getting whatever help he needed. One session wouldn't kill them and it might shed light on some issues.

JODIE DROPPED A PAYMENT off at Sam's office on the Tuesday after their interrupted date at the Supper Club. The strawberry-blond receptionist took the check without a word, wrote a receipt and was just handing it to her when Sam came in through the back door. He smiled when he saw Jodie, his cheeks creasing in a ridiculously attractive way, and she felt a wallop of guilt.

Would he look at her that way, smile at her, if he knew the truth?

"Hey, Sam," she said casually before he got to the counter, then turned on her heel and walked out the door, the little bells jingling merrily at her exit. Total shutdown, but necessary. At least until she got some perspective.

As soon as she aimed the Spitfire toward the ranch, she reached for her phone. Carmen Phillips, efficient as ever, answered on the first ring.

"I need perspective," Jodie said without identifying herself. She and Carmen had gone to law school together. They'd both landed in Vegas firms and had a habit of meeting a couple times a month for drinks and decompression.

"Shoot." Jodie knew from her absent tone that Carmen was probably still reading or making notes as she talked.

"I was involved in a DUI case two years ago. I got the charges dropped due to a procedural error."

"Good for you," Carmen said absently.

"The guy's now in prison for vehicular homicide."

"Some people never learn."

"I'm kind of getting involved with the victim's brother. More than I intended."

There was a silence. "And you're feeling guilty?" Jodie now had Carmen's full attention.

"Yes."

There was another healthy silence before Carmen said in her characteristically impatient tone, "Damn it, Jodie, think about this. I mean…come on. Think! Did you do what you were paid to do? Did you do anything illegal or unethical?"

Jodie simply exhaled instead of answering.

"Sure, it's crummy things turned out the way they

did, but unless you have an uncanny ability to foresee the future, I don't see how you could have done anything different. 'Profession—attorney.' Does that sound familiar?"

"Yes. Thanks."

"Sheesh." Carmen sounded as if she couldn't believe she'd had to give this lecture.

"Thanks," Jodie said again.

"Anything else?" Meaning that Carmen needed to get back to the nine things she was probably doing simultaneously.

"No. I'll call if there is."

"You better not have to call," Carmen warned before Jodie hung up.

She drove home feeling better. Carmen was right. What she was feeling was human, but she wasn't human. She was a lawyer.

Her lips twisted slightly.

Human. Lawyer. It didn't matter. She was very attracted to Sam, but would tread lightly. No sense screwing his life up any more than she already had.

SAM HAD ALWAYS FOUND IT odd that a school after hours didn't seem so much like a school at all. Just a big empty industrial-like space. The overhead lights were dim as he and his nephews made their way down the long hall to the counseling office, their footsteps echoing on the tile. Brighter light spilled out of the office and Sam paused in the doorway to allow Beau and Tyler to precede him into the room.

Both boys waited right inside the door and Sam had

no trouble figuring out why. The counselor, Paige, was a knockout. She also wore an engagement ring, so hopefully the guys wouldn't try to fix him up with her—although from their expressions, it looked as if they wouldn't mind taking a shot at her themselves.

"Hi," Beau said when she smiled warmly and reached over the desk to take his hand and then Tyler's, before introducing herself as Paige Mansfield.

"Sam Hyatt." Sam shook her hand, then settled into a chair. The boys also sat, their eyes never leaving her face. Perhaps this was going to go better than Sam had first anticipated.

That hope did indeed pan out. After a few awkward minutes, Beau and Tyler began to relax as Paige told them a little about her life and hobbies, and generally looked beautiful. Sam was pretty sure the beautiful part had a lot to do with his nephews' conciliatory attitude.

When she invited the three of them to talk about themselves, Beau and Tyler, in typical teen fashion, gave the abridged version of their lives, and Sam didn't do much better. Paige didn't seem to mind. She leaned back in her chair and asked a few opening questions, gathering opinions from all three of them about their present situation. She expertly guided the conversation, almost without them being aware, and Sam soon understood she was laying a base, building trust, not pushing matters too fast or too far. The boys seemed surprised when the session was over.

"That's it?" Beau asked. "You don't want us to pour out our guts about our parents and stuff?"

Paige smiled and shook her head. "If you come back,

we'll discuss some of the issues you mentioned in more detail, come up with some strategies that work for everyone," she said, smiling again, at Sam this time.

"You guys want to come back?" Sam asked before rising from his chair.

Beau shrugged. "Sure. I guess."

"I don't have a problem with it," Tyler added.

"Great. Same time next week?"

"See you then," Sam said. He left feeling that even if the sessions didn't help, they wouldn't hurt like the previous ones had. Paige had the boys talking and had subtly made the point that if people didn't communicate, they couldn't expect others to read their minds or meet their needs.

Communication. What a concept.

ON HIS WAY HOME from doing an ultrasound on a mare at the Taylor ranch, Sam did something he wouldn't have done three weeks ago, or even two weeks ago. He turned onto the Zephyr Ranch road. Just because.

No, not just because. He'd turned onto the road to check on the heifers.

Yeah. Much better. It wasn't that he wanted an excuse to see Jodie now that the damned Zephyr Valley heifers were calving with no problems, or that he wanted to find out why she had shut him down in the office the other day.

He shook his head as the main ranch house came into view. He never thought he'd be working up excuses to see Joe Barton's daughter.

Who, it turned out, wasn't home.

Shit.

But he had a long talk with Lucas, who'd come out of the ranch house when Sam had driven in, zipping up his coat and missing his ever present scarf. It had been a good talk even if Sam's thoughts had occasionally strayed elsewhere. Lucas was still sober and showing no signs of relapse, and Sam was damned proud of the man. It couldn't be easy walking away from a good twenty years of career drinking, although he'd only been nonstop soused for the past five. That was a long time to look at the world through bloodshot eyes.

Lucas told Sam that he'd just missed Jodie, who'd gone to town to do the weekly grocery shopping, so Sam asked about the heifers and the bull, killing time. Lucas answered, his attitude friendly enough, even though he kept casting quick, oddly regretful glances in the direction of the main house.

Finally Sam gave up, got in his truck and headed back to town. He had no more scheduled calls, so it was bookkeeping for him. *Whoopee.*

But he never made it to the office. Before he reached town, his cell rang, and less than a minute later he hit the accelerator hard and turned onto the highway leading to Elko instead of the back road to the clinic.

CHAPTER ELEVEN

THE GROCERY STORE WAS Jodie's last stop after a visit to the garage Lucas had recommended. He'd assured her the place was capable of servicing the Spitfire. Not just anyone got to mess with her baby, but she did need to have the car maintained before the drive back to Las Vegas.

By the time she'd finally searched out the final item on Margarite's list—agave nectar, which was like a honey rather than a juice as she'd first thought, there was a long line at the checkout counter. As usual, there were two clerks when they needed four, so Jodie read magazine headlines until she finally pushed her cart up to the register and the lady in the pink smock began scanning items. Jodie loaded groceries into plastic bags as they tumbled down the conveyer toward the end of the long counter, trying to keep up with the clerk.

She was focused on sorting produce from dry goods when she heard Sam's name, and glanced over her shoulder at the other counter. A woman she didn't recognize was waiting for the clerk to load her last bag into a cart.

"Horrifying," the woman said into her cell phone before pausing to listen.

Jodie's groceries were piling up and she turned her attention back to bagging them while eavesdropping on the call behind her, her heart beating faster. What had happened to Sam?

"Yes, Doc Hyatt had a bad time of it. Jim said he'd never seen him so… Yes, Jim's still there, cleaning up the wreck…." The woman's voice faded as she pushed her cart away from the counter and out the door.

Jodie felt numb as she continued to jam items into bags with no rhyme or reason. Perishable, nonperishable. Who cared?

"Have you heard anything about an accident?" she asked the checker. The woman just shook her head as she scanned the last few items.

Well, something had happened.

Jodie went to the credit scanner and ran her card while the woman loaded the bags in the cart. Impatiently, Jodie punched buttons until the receipt finally snaked out of the machine. She snatched the long strip of paper, then grabbed the handle of the cart and wheeled it to the door.

Doc Hyatt had a bad time of it.

And if Jim, whoever he was, was still clearing up the wreck, the accident must have just happened. Jodie made her way across the lot and had to slam on the brakes when a car she didn't see sailed past her on the street. She forced herself to look both directions, twice, before proceeding.

Not the boys. Please don't let anything have happened to the boys. Sam didn't need more pain in his life.

She drove straight to his house, where, thankfully,

the vet truck was parked in front of the clinic. But she had no idea if his private vehicle was there, and when she headed past the clinic to the driveway to his home, she saw that the little white truck the boys drove was definitely absent.

Please don't let it be the wreck Jim was cleaning up.

Jodie parked next to the back door, and as she got out of the car she saw movement at the kitchen window. Okay. Someone was there. A second later Sam opened the door, frowning when he saw her.

"Are you all right?" Jodie blurted. He looked okay. A bit worn around the edges, but not devastated.

"Yeah. Why?"

"I heard something at the grocery store…." He was staring at her oddly.

"Heard what?"

She moistened her lips. "Heard wrong, I guess. I thought there was some kind of trouble. A car wreck."

Understanding dawned across his features. "I had to put down some horses involved in a highway accident. It was…ugly, to say the least." He gestured at the blood-stained clothing kicked into a pile in the corner of the mudroom.

Jodie looked away from the bloody shirt and jeans, pressing her fingertips to her forehead. "I was afraid it might have involved the boys or…something…." Her voice faltered. "You know?"

"So you came over here to make sure they were all right?"

"And you."

"Me." Sam gave his head a slight shake, then opened the door leading from the mudroom into the kitchen. She followed him inside the warm house and he closed the door again.

"You want a drink?"

"I could use one," Jodie said honestly. She looked around at the old-fashioned kitchen, which was exceptionally neat for having three males in the house.

"Jodie…explain something to me." Sam went to the cabinet and pulled out a bottle of red wine, which he held up for approval. Jodie automatically nodded. She was not all that interested in vintages at the moment. "What's going on between us?"

Yes. What?

"I mean, you could have called, but you showed up in person."

"Yes, I did." Jodie ran her fingers down the silk scarf she wore. Yes, she had indeed come in person. She'd wanted to see Sam, assure herself that all was well.

"But you've been avoiding me for the past few days." He pulled down two wineglasses from an open shelf over the sink, inspected them, then set them on the counter.

"You did reject me," she pointed out, wincing inwardly as she spoke. *Oh, good. Clutch at straws. Excellent strategy.*

Sam uncorked the wine without responding, apparently thinking her point was not worth addressing. Jodie pushed her hair behind her ears, watching the muscles of his back move under his shirt.

"I don't think we're interested in the same thing," she

finally blurted in a most unlawyerly fashion. Sam turned then, and from the way he looked at her, she realized she could be mistaken about that.

"What are *you* interested in?" he asked.

"Something short-term and physical," she said without hesitation, thinking that might put him off. "I'm too involved with my career for anything else." Not the total truth, but her statement had elements of truth.

His lips twitched before he poured the wine. "Yeah, I have a big problem having sex with a hot woman, no strings attached."

"I think you do," Jodie said, a stubborn note in her voice.

"Why?"

"Because you want to be a good role model for the boys."

Sam handed her a glass, then lightly touched it with his own in a silent toast. "The boys have encouraged me to get a life so they can have their own."

"Oh." Well, that argument was shot to hell. "That's happy news," Jodie deadpanned.

"I'd kind of like to start doing that," he said. "Getting a life."

A slow anticipatory tingle went down Jodie's spine. "I have Margarite's groceries."

"Anything perishable?"

"Yes."

"Pretty cold right now. They'd probably be fine in the car."

"Uh-huh." Jodie didn't seem to be able to tear her eyes away from Sam's.

Was it right to do this? Without telling him that she'd once defended Colin Craig? Kept the man from going to prison for that third DUI?

Telling Sam wouldn't help either of them. It would devastate him. She couldn't change the past, only regret it, and that wasn't going to bring Dave Hyatt back, give the twins their parents again. But she could make Sam feel pretty damned good, and maybe by connecting with him…maybe she could do herself some good, too.

"Where are the boys?" she asked.

"Gone until late." Sam's gaze was intense. "They went to Elko with some of their teammates."

"I thought that after last week they'd be grounded forever."

"So did I," Sam said. "However…" He reached out to wipe a droplet of wine from her lower lip with the pad of his thumb, making her knees feel ridiculously weak.

"However?" she prompted, her voice almost failing her.

"We went to family counseling this week, and I discovered that I have control issues. The counselor mentioned that trying to control things in order to feel safe was a normal response to my…situation." Sam took a swallow of wine. "She also mentioned that it's futile."

"I know." Jodie spoke softly. Her words hung for a moment before she continued. "I have a tendency to try to control too much, too."

"Maybe the solution is to just let go."

"You think?"

Sam put his glass on the counter, his gaze traveling

down her body, lingering on her breasts, then coming back up to her mouth. "Yeah. In a short-term, very physical way."

Jodie reached up to pull the silk scarf from around her neck, draping it over the closest kitchen chair. "So are you going to kiss me, or what?"

"I'd really like to experience 'or what.'"

"Well, here's your chance," Jodie said, giving in and bringing her hands up to cup the sides of his face and pull his mouth down to hers. She rose up on her toes, trying to press closer, needing to feel his heat, his hardness in order to wipe the remaining doubts from her mind.

His mouth moved away from hers and she murmured in protest, then sucked in a breath as his lips trailed down her neck to the hollow of her shoulder, making odd little tremors shoot through her. She lifted her hands to his face, reclaiming his mouth before running her palms down his back to his ass. And what an ass.

"I, uh, haven't had sex in a long time," she finally said, her voice barely audible.

"How do you feel about ending your dry spell?" Sam asked.

She laughed in spite of herself, loving how his body felt against her own. "It's time," she said.

Sam swung her up into his arms and carried her down the hall, past an open office door and into his bedroom. His bed was a mess, all rumpled sheets and tangled blankets. Jodie could imagine him crawling out of it at all hours of the night in order to go on an emergency call.

The thought froze her up as he set her on her feet and smoothed her hair back over her shoulders before bringing his forehead down to touch hers. He'd better not get any calls tonight.

Her fingers were a bit unsteady as she worked the plain white buttons on his chambray shirt through the holes. The sleeves were rolled up to his forearms, so when Jodie finally pushed the fabric off his shoulders, it fell freely to the floor. His chest was solid, all taut muscles lightly covered with reddish hair. Who would have thought she'd fall for a Viking?

Sam sucked in a breath as she went for his jeans, but he didn't make a move as she undid the top button, then put a hand on either side of the opening and pulled in opposite directions, springing the buttons free and releasing him.

"You don't wear underwear?" she asked, surprised and more than a little impressed, both at his bravado and at...him.

"I showered when I got back from the call, and didn't bother."

She ran a hand over the length of him and felt him throb in response. "I like this look. You should consider making it part of your personal style."

Sam reached down and caught her hands as he stepped out of the jeans, then used his feet to peel off his wool socks. And there he stood. Male, totally gorgeous. Better than her imagination, which had been pretty good.

"I cannot believe the women of this town are not all over you," she said.

"There's only one woman I want all over me," Sam growled, "and I'd like her a lot more naked than she is now."

"Okay," Jodie said simply, spreading her arms, inviting him to take charge, which he did.

"Is this a component of the 'or what' you were talking about?"

Jodie laughed and shrugged out of her coat, which she tossed on the heap she'd made of Sam's clothes. "It can be."

She didn't laugh after that. She gasped a few times as Sam slowly undressed her, following his hands with his lips, and she moaned when he took off her panties and his finger strayed exactly where she wanted it. But she definitely wanted more than a finger, and Sam was happy to oblige.

His comment about experiencing "or what" shot through her brain as he entered her. *Oh. My. Gosh.* This was definitely "or what." She couldn't come up with adequate words to describe how it felt having him inside of her.

He seemed to feel the same about her. His expression was one of awe as he pushed himself in to the hilt. And then he started to move.

Maybe she hadn't had sex in a while, but she had never had sex like this. She would have remembered.

Sam covered her mouth with his and Jodie pushed her hands up into his thick blond hair, holding him as he plunged into her. When she came, she cried out against his lips, arching and throbbing. He was only seconds behind her.

After he'd collapsed, Jodie ran her hands lightly over his broad back, trying desperately to catch her breath. She felt him smile against her shoulder.

"Was it good for you?" he asked whimsically. He'd have to be dense to have thought otherwise, and Sam was not dense.

"Not bad."

He raised his head, smiling at her, looking more relaxed than she'd ever seen him. With his longish blond hair falling down on his forehead, he looked almost like a beach bum. A very delicious beach bum.

"Can you do better?" he asked.

"Give me a few minutes and I'll show you."

JODIE'S PARENTS WERE DUE home in a week and a half. She planned to spend a few days with them, then drive back to Vegas just before her sabbatical officially ended. Sam had no idea what would ultimately happen between the two of them—whether short-term and physical would evolve into something else—but for now he was going to make the most of this small window of time he had with Jodie. She was of the same mind.

"Sam," Beau called. "Emergency."

He went into the living room where Beau was holding the phone out. "Yeah," Sam said into the receiver.

"Margarite is gone for the evening and I have the place to myself. This may not happen again before my folks come back."

"Be right there," Sam said, wondering how Jodie had talked Margarite into leaving for a night. All expenses paid weekend in Elko, perhaps? He put the phone back in the cradle, then went into the mudroom to grab his canvas coat and shove his feet into his barn boots.

"Barton ranch?" Tyler asked when Sam went for his keys.

Sam did a quick double take. "Yeah."

Without another word, Tyler turned back to the pizza he was cutting, but Sam saw that the kid was smiling. There was *no way* the boys could be aware of what had happened between him and Jodie, but somehow they were.

Perhaps because he was ridiculously cheerful. Vets were not cheerful during calving season. They were tired. He was that, too, but not necessarily because of late night emergencies.

"I'll be home by midnight," he said, still playing the game even if he wasn't fooling anyone. And he would be home by midnight, even if it killed him.

Forty minutes later, Jodie met him at the ranch house door, pulling his mouth down to meet hers before he was all the way inside. Sam wrapped his arms around her, lifting her feet off the ground, his lips staying on hers, kissing her deeply as he kicked the door shut behind him. Once he put her back on the ground, they made their way to the bedroom, leaving a trail of clothing that Margarite was going to find rather interesting if they didn't retrieve them before she got home.

"I have to be home by midnight...one o'clock at the latest," he said as they fell naked into Jodie's bed.

She didn't answer, but instead dropped kisses over his chest, her clever hands doing things that made him believe time would not be an issue. If she continued what she was doing right now, their evening would soon be over.

So he reached down for her, dragged her up the length of his body until he could kiss her. She smiled and shook her head. This time Sam surrendered, lying back and letting her have her way with him. And she was better than he'd thought, stopping at just the right moment when he was on the brink.

"Your turn," she said with a wicked smile.

He obliged and discovered that Jodie didn't have his self-control—or perhaps he didn't have her timing. Regardless, she didn't seem at all repentant about letting go when she did; she laughed and pushed her hair back from her forehead when Sam growled something about leaving him in the dust. He rolled over onto his back and positioned her on top of him, enjoying the way her eyes first widened and then drifted shut as he lowered her onto him. He made himself last as long as he could, really wanting her to come again. Jodie obliged, letting out a gasp that caught in her throat just before Sam emptied himself into her.

She stretched out on top of his damp body, tucking her head under his chin, and he closed his arms around her. "Are you surprised at how good this is?" she asked.

"A little. But I'm not going to question it." He ran a hand over her back, loving the feel of her silky skin. This was more than just sex, more than something short-term and physical—at least at his end. Jodie...it was hard to read her.

She nodded at his response, but offered no reply. Sam was okay with that.

"My folks will be home soon."

Sam let out a breath. "Yeah."

Jodie rolled off him, onto her back, dropping her arm over her forehead. "I must confess I am not looking forward to giving my father the ranch report."

Sam turned his head to glance at her profile, or what he could see of it. "What's the deal with your dad, Jodie? It sounds like you're afraid of him."

Her half-shut eyes snapped open. "No. It's just that he's a perfectionist and he expects people to live up to his standards. When they don't, well, he can be kind of unforgiving."

"Even with you?" Sam's parents had set standards for him and Dave, but he couldn't remember a time when they'd been unforgiving.

"It's just the way he is," Jodie said, shifting to her side so she could look into Sam's eyes. "It'll pass." He frowned and she explained, "My father has always wanted me to be the best. When I make the grade, he's in the front of the cheering section. When I don't...well, he pretty much withdraws until I do something up to par to make up for it."

"So in other words," Sam said coolly, "your father is big into emotional blackmail."

Jodie pushed up onto her elbow. "That is *not* what I said."

Sam tucked her hair behind her ears. "It's what it sounds like."

She let out a sigh. "I guess you have to be part of

the family to understand, but it worked for me. I was always striving to be the best because of my father, and it's served me well in life. Toughened me up. Prepared me for the real world and all that."

It sounded sick to Sam, but right now he wasn't going to waste time on psychoanalysis. He wrapped his arms around Jodie and pulled her against him, kissing her deeply and trying to convey that no matter what, he liked her just the way she was.

JODIE LAY STILL as Sam slipped out of bed at eleven-thirty. Knowing he had to get back to town, she closed her eyes, drawing in his scent from the sheets and very much wanting to drag him back to bed for another round.

He dressed in the dark, his movements quick and sure, making Jodie wonder how many times in his life he'd been called out of bed for a veterinary emergency. After his boots were on, he came over to her side. Jodie rolled languidly onto her back.

"I wish I could stay."

"I know," she agreed. "And I'm fighting the urge to pull you back down here with me." She could see from the way he was looking at her that he was tempted. "Have I mentioned that it turns me on making love to guys who are almost dressed?"

"Good thing I'm *entirely* dressed."

"Yeah."

He sat on the edge of the bed and put a hand on either side of her face, leaning in for a long, deep kiss.

"Keep that up and you won't be entirely dressed for long," she murmured against his lips. "You'd better get out of here while you can."

He laughed softly, kissed her again and then stood.

"See you around, Sam."

"Get some sleep," he said before he started for the door.

Jodie curled onto her side, flexing her tired muscles. *Yes. Sleep.* The next time she opened her eyes, gray light was coming in through the windows and she could hear Margarite out in the kitchen. Margarite, who must have come home instead of staying in town with her sister after the movie as she'd planned.

"I passed Sam as I was driving home last night. Did he have an emergency here?" the housekeeper asked when Jodie came into the kitchen.

"Yes."

"I guess that's why your panties are under the coffee table?" Margarite gave Jodie an arch look, then disappeared into the pantry.

Jodie clapped a hand to her forehead and went into the living room, where her panties were indeed under the coffee table. Time for damage control.

CHAPTER TWELVE

JODIE WAITED UNTIL Margarite had done the few dishes and was settled with her crossword puzzle book and coffee before she opened the lines of communication.

"Margarite? I have a favor to ask." She spoke in her brisk lawyer voice and Margarite's eyebrows rose at her tone. Jodie immediately shifted gears.

"I'm sorry. I didn't mean to sound like that. Anyway, as you've figured out, Sam and I are..." Wow. *Sam and I are lovers?* That sounded dumb. *Seeing each other?* Naked, maybe. They weren't dating. They were sleeping together. "We're..."

"No kidding," Margarite said bluntly.

"Anyway, I would appreciate it if you didn't give my dad a heart attack by telling him about us."

That honor was reserved for her. Or maybe this was another secret she'd keep. The one she was keeping now was still pushing its way into her conscience, nagging at her. No matter how she tried to beat it into submission, it popped up, telling her that she was making love to Sam under false pretenses.

"I wouldn't dream of it," Margarite said. Then she

picked up her pencil and started working on the puzzle. When she didn't look up for several minutes, Jodie decided to make a retreat.

"See what you can do to keep Lucas on, would you?"

Jodie turned back at Margarite's unexpected request, her heartbeat doing an odd skip when she saw the worried expression on the housekeeper's face. "You bet. And if Dad won't listen to reason, Sam can help Lucas get on somewhere else."

Margarite gave a quick smile. "Thanks, Jodie. I'd appreciate it."

JODIE AND SAM GOT together two more times before her parents came home, and both occasions ended with veterinary emergencies. Sam assured her this wasn't the norm, but Jodie, in an odd way, felt it was no more than she deserved—maybe because she loved making love to Sam, yet knew it couldn't develop into anything else. Not without her confessing her part in his brother's death, and she couldn't handle doing that. When she thought back to the celebration she'd had after getting Craig off, she felt queasy. To tell Sam about what she'd done... She couldn't do it, and the crazy thing was, it was more for his sake than for hers.

Margarite put a prime rib in the oven the morning of Joe and Nadine Barton's return to the ranch. The housekeeper was worried about Lucas, Jodie was worried about bringing her father up to speed. All in all it was a tense morning for both of them. Only Lucas seemed to have a come-what-may attitude. He serenely went about his business, fueling up the tractor and feeding the herd. Jodie watched him roll back in from the pasture as she pulled the ranch Suburban out of the garage to pick up her parents. She hoped Lucas would be driving the tractor in from the field tomorrow. With Joe there was no telling.

Jodie obsessed the entire way to Elko, and was terrifically relieved to see her father actually smiling when he entered the waiting area at the Elko airport. He also had that spring-loaded look that meant he was ready to get to work. Now.

"Jodie!" Nadine Barton launched herself at her daughter, catching her in a huge hug that left Jodie breathless and laughing.

"I'm so glad you're back," Jodie said when her mom released her. "What a great haircut."

Nadine put a hand up to her pale blond hair. "The stylist's name is Fabio and he's stunning. I wish I could go back for a trim, but your father says it isn't practical." Her eyes were brimming with humor.

Joe looked heavenward, but smiled instead of scowling. Apparently, time away had done him some good. "I missed you. Dad, you look great." Jodie gave him a quick hug.

"It's good to be home," he said, returning the embrace quickly and self-consciously. "How's the ranch?"

It was Jodie's turn to roll her eyes. "It's still there. I want to hear about your trip first." Her strategy was to wait until they were home and Joe had bourbon in his hand before discussing what had happened at the ranch. That way, instead of chomping at the bit to get home and see what kind of imagined devastation awaited, he could immediately see that everything was indeed fine. Maybe not as fine as when he'd left, but acceptable.

Joe did his best to derail her plan, peppering her with questions before they reached the parking lot, but fortunately Nadine wanted to talk about the trip, and told him that Mike could fill him in when they got to the ranch. He'd know more than Jodie.

"I have a lot to tell you," Jodie agreed. *You have no idea how much.* "We'll have a sitdown right after lunch. Margarite has really outdone herself cooking for your return."

"Will Mike be around when we get back?" her father asked.

"No, but I can fill you in."

Nadine took over the conversation then and Jodie listened to her talk about Greece and southern Italy with half an ear, while she reviewed her battle strategy. She had two objectives—to keep her dad calm and to keep Lucas at the ranch. It was simply a matter of presentation.

Of course, Joe wanted to take a ranch tour as soon as he set foot on the property, but Jodie managed to get him into the office while Margarite put lunch on the table and her mother freshened up. Joe poured a glass of bourbon, neat, and held up the bottle. As much as she could use a shot of courage, Jodie shook her head.

"Some things happened on the ranch while you were gone."

Instant frown.

"First of all," Jodie continued coolly, "Mike went to visit his family and didn't come back."

The frown deepened, but Joe appeared remarkably calm when he said, "How did you handle that?"

"Lucas Reynolds finished rehab and was looking for a job. I hired him out of desperation."

"I guess you *must* have been desperate," Joe growled as all signs of calm acceptance evaporated. "Lucas Reynolds!"

"Dad. He's done a fine job. He's helped me through some tight spots."

Joe appeared unconvinced as he considered his drink for a moment. "What tight spots?"

"Does Mom know you're still drinking bourbon?" Jodie asked, instead of answering his question.

He glanced up at her. "I keep it to one a day." He gestured with the glass. "This is my one."

"Which is more than Lucas has. He goes to AA meetings in Wesley every Tuesday night, but other than that, he rarely leaves the ranch." Jodie paused for a moment. "I want you to keep him on, Dad."

"What tight spots?"

"Feeding, calving. We lost part of the herd when a culvert drifted shut, and he knew exactly why they were missing, and found them. He's barely taken a day off and he's never taken a day off from feeding."

"When exactly did Mike quit?"

"A week after you left. He found a job in Idaho."

"Then he knew he was going to quit before I left."

"Probably."

"That son of a bitch."

"Will you keep Lucas?" When he didn't answer immediately, Jodie played her trump. "He and Margarite may be…involved. I think if you lose one, you'll lose both. I'm not positive, but…" She shrugged.

Joe let out an exasperated breath. "Okay, I'll give him a trial. That's as much as I can promise, since he screwed up the last time he was here. Anything else I need to know about?"

One down, and her father was once again relatively calm. Would her luck hold?

"Bronson got out of the pasture shortly after you left, and was spooked into a piece of farm equipment. He was badly cut."

"What?!" The drink slammed down on the mahogany desk. "Why didn't you—"

Jodie cut him off, her voice rising for the first time. "I think you know why. What good would it have done? You would have driven Mom crazy and there wasn't a thing you could do about it. He'll have some scarring on his chest, but if you had seen his injury, you'd appreciate just how well he's healed."

Joe took a couple paces to the window and stared out. "I'll take a look after lunch." His relaxed expression was long gone. "Anything *else?*" he demanded grimly.

"We've had seventeen live calves and all the heifers are doing fine. The only loss was a stillborn twin."

"Lucas was good with calving," Joe admitted grudgingly. "How much did Eriksson charge for the horse?"

"He wasn't the one who sewed up Bronson. Sam Hyatt did."

"Sam—"

"He also treated a bull for hardware disease."

"Hardware..." For a moment her father simply stared at her.

"Sometimes cattle swallow bits of metal and—"

"I know what hardware disease is. I'm working on the part where you had Hyatt out here instead of Eriksson. What in the *hell* were you thinking?"

"I was thinking Sam was the only vet I could talk into coming out here. I had to beg, Dad."

"You begged Sam Hyatt."

Among other things. "Yes."

Joe shook his head, then pressed his lips together tightly. "We'll talk about this later."

"Dr. Eriksson was out of the office for two weeks. He wasn't available, so I did the only thing I could to save the horse."

"Maybe it would have been better if he'd died," Joe snapped.

Jodie turned and walked out of the room. It was the only thing she could do when her father got like this.

Jodie and her mother ate lunch together without Joe, who was touring the ranch, and Nadine practically glowed as she continued to describe the trip. It was the first time in a decade she'd had her husband's full attention and she'd loved every minute. Meanwhile Jodie was thinking, *Oh, there will be hell to pay for the Sam Hyatt issue.*

"I wish your father could have joined us," Nadine said, as if reading Jodie's thoughts. "But you know how he is."

Yes. Stewing about Jodie's poor decision making. But eventually Joe did come back into the house, and Jodie was impressed when he put an arm around his wife and gave her a quick, affectionate squeeze before he faced his daughter and the deep freeze set in.

"I need to take care of a few things online," Jodie said, excusing herself. She was almost at the office when Lucas came into the living room, his battered felt hat in one hand. He nodded nervously at Joe, who sucked in a breath and nodded back.

"I have some bad news." He spoke to Joe, but his eyes were on Jodie. "One of the bulls is dead."

"Which one?" Joe asked in a frighteningly calm tone.

"The black one from Oklahoma."

THE ENTIRE FAMILY BUNDLED up and went out to the pasture, even Nadine, who rarely set foot outside the house except for her morning walk and to paint landscapes or flowers.

The bull was indeed dead, lying on his side, eyes rolled back in his head.

"He'd recovered," Jodie said faintly, causing her dad to give her a sharp look.

"Did Sam Hyatt treat this bull?"

Jodie rounded on her father. “He didn’t die from what Sam treated him for.”

“How in the hell do you know that?” Color flooded into Joe’s face, and his voice was like a volcanic eruption. “I still cannot believe you had *Sam Hyat*t out here treating my animals.”

“They would have died if he hadn’t,” Jodie shouted back.

“Well, it looks like one died, anyway.” Joe’s voice dripped sarcasm.

“He was the only vet who would come out here, and you’re damned lucky he did.”

“There had to be other options.”

“Joe,” Nadine said, “be reasonable.” She was close to tears, but both Joe and Jodie ignored her plea.

“There weren’t,” Jodie stated flatly. She had done the only thing possible. “He saved Bronson and he saved more than one calf for you because your wonder cowboy Mike refused to come back to work for you.”

Joe’s mouth clamped into a tight line.

“Come on, Dad. What else could I do?”

“Called Eriksson. Did it never occur to you that incompetent son of a bitch Hyatt might screw up and kill my bull?”

“The bull recovered.”

“He’s dead! And it’s your fault!”

Enough. Jodie’s stomach was in a tight knot, but she’d had it.

“No. It’s *your* fault for alienating all the vets in the

area. More than one of them told you Sam had followed the proper course of action with the horse. But you couldn't accept that. Someone had to take the blame."

Joe glared at her, as if he couldn't believe she was arguing this point, then turned and stalked back toward the ranch house. Nadine put her arms around Jodie, making peace as always.

"He'll come around."

Jodie gently stepped out of her mother's embrace. "He shouldn't have to come around. He should be able to see that I did what I had to do."

"The bull and the horse...that's not what he expected when he came back."

"It's a ranch, Mom. These things happen." And, boy, did they. "If he can't accept that, he needs to find another retirement gig." Jodie shook her head. "I need to take care of this."

"What are you going to do?" Nadine asked as they started for the house.

"I'm going to do what I should have done before. I'm calling Eriksson."

Dr. Eriksson was free, since it was a weekend, and he flew in later that day, as Jodie arranged. The autopsy was going to cost her a bundle, and there was always the chance that the vet would say, yes, Sam had been negligent. But there was a chance he wouldn't, and Jodie wanted this matter put to rest.

Joe paced the fence as Eriksson cut into his prize bull. Thankfully, it was warm enough outside that the animal had not frozen solid. It didn't take long before the vet shook his head. "It had nothing to do with the magnet," he said, pulling the bullet-shaped piece of metal out of the animal's rumen. "In fact, it was exactly the right treatment."

Jodie, who was not watching for obvious reasons, felt a swell of vindication. *There.*

Joe wouldn't accept the vet's conclusion. "Well, then why the hell is this animal dead?"

"I'll have to take a liver swab, but right now, I'd say red water disease."

"Shouldn't Hyatt have caught that?"

Eriksson shook his head. "Don't see how he could have. It wouldn't have shown up in blood tests and has nothing to do with the metal in the rumen."

Jodie had heard enough. She left the pens and headed back to the warmth of the house. Half an hour after Dr. Eriksson's plane left the runway, Jodie sought out Joe in his den.

"Well?" She wanted him to tell her he'd been wrong, but knew by the stubborn look on his face that he wasn't giving in.

"You made me look foolish, having Sam Hyatt back on the place. I mean, can you imagine how much fun the locals are having with this? And then he kills my bull?"

"He did not kill your bull."

"I'll wait for the blood test results before I believe that." Joe ran a hand over the back of his neck and Jodie saw that his features were as tight, if not tighter, than before he'd left on vacation. All the hell she'd been through was for nothing…except for connecting with

Sam. That was worthwhile. Maybe this was simply the price she had to pay for finding a decent man to spend some time with.

Joe wasn't finished. "The horse I understand," he said grimly, "but Eriksson would have flown in for everything else."

"Not the bull. I called him. He was on vacation."

"And due back the next day. I checked! He would have taken over. He told me. You had no business bringing Sam Hyatt onto this property for more than that one emergency."

Would it never end? "I did the best I could under the circumstances."

"You could have done a hell of a lot better than you did."

Jodie felt the instinctive tightening in the pit of her stomach that always followed those words. She was not good enough. Be the best or don't bother.

She was thirty years old, no longer a girl who needed to please her father, so it pissed her off that the words still stung.

"If you didn't plan to respect what's important to me, you shouldn't have volunteered to take over the ranch."

She opened her mouth to answer, and was surprised that she couldn't find any words. She was a lawyer, for heaven's sake. Words were her business. Finally, she just shook her head and walked out of the office and down the hall to her room, where she finished the packing she'd started that morning.

There was no question of Joe coming in to make nice.

That wasn't the way he operated. And since her mother had no idea of what had just happened, she would hopefully assume that Jodie was simply leaving a bit early, anxious to get back to her job.

But she'd had it. She would not be back at the ranch anytime soon. She'd meet her mom in Vegas for shopping and that would be enough family for her. She was so damned sick of feeling like a failure for things out of her control. She couldn't help it if some other student was better than her and she couldn't help it if Joe had managed to get himself blackballed with every vet in northeastern Nevada.

Her hands were practically shaking by the time she finished shoving stuff into her two suitcases. She lugged them through the house and out the mudroom door to the Spitfire.

"You won't be here for dinner?" Margarite asked.

Jodie smiled calmly. "No. I thought I'd better hit the road. There's supposed to be a storm coming in."

"Day after tomorrow."

"And I want to be safely in Vegas when it hits."

Margarite gave her a shrewd look. "Yes," she said ironically. "Better safe than sorry."

Jodie stowed her luggage, then went back to the house to find her mother and say goodbye.

"You're leaving early," Nadine said, a note of sadness in her voice.

"I have some unexpected loose ends I need to wrap up."

Nadine had watched the fireworks between Jodie and

her father too often not to know what was really going on, although this was the first time Jodie had refused to placate Joe.

No. She might be a failure in his eyes, but for once she wasn't going to do anything to rectify his opinion.

Joe came into the library then, his expression still stormy. "You're leaving?"

"I have to get back," she said in a clipped voice.

"I thought you were going to spend a couple days here with your mom."

Oh, yes. This was so like him. Make it look like she was falling short no matter what she did.

"Mom and I can hook up in Vegas."

"Jodie—" There was no hint of remorse in his voice.

"Look, Dad. I have to get back." *I did the best I could, and as usual, it wasn't good enough.*

"When will we see you again?" he asked in a way that made her wonder if he even cared about the answer. It would be less painful for everyone if he didn't.

"I don't know."

And Jodie meant it. She was damned tired of feeling like a failure when she knew she wasn't. Why couldn't her father accept her, warts and all? Why did he have to beat blame into her before he could forgive her? Before he could love her again?

Enough.

CHAPTER THIRTEEN

JODIE DROVE TO SAM'S place on autopilot. By some miracle, his truck was parked beside the clinic. He was there. Finally something had gone right today.

She entered the clinic to see Sam behind the counter. The strawberry-blond receptionist who didn't seem to think much of Jodie was nowhere in sight.

"What happened?" Sam asked.

"How do you know something happened?"

"The reveal-nothing look on your face."

He was beginning to know her too well. "The bull died."

"The bull I treated?"

"Yeah." Sam came around the counter, a grim look on his face. "It wasn't your fault," Jodie said quickly. "I had Eriksson fly in and do an autopsy. He totally exonerated you, but Dad's still…being Dad."

"I can imagine," he muttered. "Am I going to get sued?"

"If you do, I'll defend you. Pro bono."

She thought Sam might smile, but he didn't, probably because the scenario wasn't out of the realm of possibility.

"What did Eriksson say?"

"Red water disease."

"Shit."

"He said there was no reason you should have caught it."

Sam nodded, looking none too happy. "So what now?" he asked, finally reaching out to fold her into his arms, where she'd wanted to be from the instant she'd walked into the office. She returned the embrace, splaying her fingers over the solid muscles of his back.

"Head off to my other life."

"Right now?"

She glanced through the window at her packed car. "Yeah."

"Why don't you leave tomorrow?"

"Sam, putting it off isn't going to—"

He cut her words off with a kiss, and when he lifted his head, she wasn't certain what point she was trying to make. "I want one last afternoon. Okay?"

"The boys—"

"Won't be home until after seven-thirty. Think of it as a long goodbye."

When he put it that way… "All right."

"I have one call to make. Do you want to come?"

"Yeah, maybe I would," she said with a wavering smile.

He put his hand on the back of her head and buried his face in her hair. "Sorry about your dad."

Jodie went with Sam to see about some goats. She played with a litter of fuzzy brown puppies that had come out of the barn to greet them, while Sam did whatever it was he'd come to do. Jodie nearly died of a cuteness overdose before getting back into the truck, and she hated saying no to the offer of a puppy of her very own, but for sanity's sake had to. A puppy and a Vegas condo were not a good mix.

Sam patted the seat next to him after starting the engine, and Jodie scooted over, fastening the middle belt around her. Sam held up his phone and hit the power button. Merry chimes sounded.

"I'm off duty," he said.

"It's about time."

They made love during the afternoon while the boys were at school, and then Jodie did something she almost never did, and fell asleep in the daytime, content to be in Sam's arms. Tomorrow she'd be alone again, so she was going to savor every moment she had with him. After today, their affair—for want of a better word—would be over, because she was heading back to her old life, and she was not going to encourage Sam to visit her in Vegas.

If her father couldn't forgive her for a bull...well, then how would Sam ever forgive her for what she'd done to him?

WHEN THREE O'CLOCK ROLLED around, the end of school and the beginning of basketball practice, Sam roused Jodie, who'd dozed off in his arms. She smiled sleepily and he brushed the hair out of her eyes, loving the warm feeling of their bodies pressed together.

Neither had asked "what now?" because they both knew what was going to happen in the immediate future. Jodie would go off to Vegas, he would stay here.

The next step was a mystery, but he suspected that it was going to involve a few trips to Vegas to see Jodie when he could manage the time. Maybe he wouldn't work so many weekends. Maybe he'd have to take on a partner.

"Anxious to get back to work?" he asked.

"I am." She ran her hand over the muscles of his shoulder. His body took that as an incentive to get busy again. "Don't fight it," Jodie said with a laugh, her hand dropping down to stroke him with the palm of her hand.

It was official, he thought as he pulled her up on top of him, loving the way she welcomed him with her body, the way they fit together so perfectly. He just couldn't get enough of her. Maybe it was because she was such a surprise to him after she'd dropped her protective facade. Or maybe he was just falling in love with her. He strongly suspected the latter and he liked the feeling.

When Jodie finally collapsed on top of him, after letting out a long, shuddering sigh of release, Sam wrapped his arms around her and held her until he slipped out of her. Only then did she roll off onto her back, smiling as she closed her eyes. Sam studied her, hating that in a matter of hours things would change. She'd be back in her life and he'd be here, surrogate father and overworked vet.

"I guess we haven't talked about what happens after this," Sam said, propping his head on his elbow. "So what happens after this?"

JODIE STARED UP AT THE ceiling, wishing he hadn't asked that question. "I don't know." But she did. She wasn't going to let herself fall for him, so she would have to keep her distance. Stay far, far away from Wesley. Obviously, short-term and physical were not working out as planned.

"Do you still view what we have as transitory?"

"That's how I have to view it." She spoke adamantly, knowing he wouldn't understand why, but needing to get the point across that things had to end.

"Would you do me a favor, Jodie?"

"What?" she asked in a low voice, still staring upward.

"Keep your options…about us…open."

"I don't know if I can."

Instead of pushing the point, or asking why, Sam simply changed the subject. "When we did our counseling session this week, Paige told us to work on communication. Real communication."

He was talking about them, him and her, but Jodie took advantage of the opening to redirect the conversation. "You weren't communicating with the boys before?"

For a moment she thought he was going to persevere and try to talk about their future, their communication, but after a brief hesitation, he said, "There were topics we avoided. I thought I was protecting them by not bringing up their parents, but the boys seemed relieved to talk." Sam laid his head back on the pillow and Jodie rolled so that they were eye to eye.

"How was it for *you*? The talking?" Jodie had to

know. She had to know how much pain she'd caused him. Inadvertent or not, she had a measure of responsibility here.

"To tell you the truth, I hadn't realized how deep down I'd pushed some of this in order to be strong for the boys. Dave and I were almost as close as Beau and Tyler. It was hell to lose him… I still miss him so much."

Jodie remained silent. What could she possibly say? I'm so sorry? In more ways than you can imagine?

"I guess I still retain a lot of anger, and I need to acknowledge it so I can deal with it."

"Yes," Jodie agreed faintly. Anger. Her fingers, which had been lightly curled on the sheet, tightened into a fist. Sam dropped an arm over her and drew her closer, but at that moment Jodie wanted space. Room to breathe, to think. She felt a wave of heat and nausea.

"Are you all right?"

"I…I'm sorry this happened, Sam."

"Yeah. It sucked. Still does."

Thankfully, Sam lapsed into silence, and Jodie made a conscious effort to relax her taut muscles. She shut her eyes as if to sleep and Sam took the hint, pulling her close, cradling her against his body. Jodie felt a tremendous weight of guilt. He wouldn't be with her now if she'd told him the truth. What they had together, what she had secretly come to treasure, was all a lie. An illusion that would evaporate once the truth was exposed.

As she felt him relax against her, his breathing becoming more even, she knew what was going to happen, what she had to do.

He was going to hate her for being a flake rather than a liar.

SAM HADN'T EXPECTED to fall asleep, or to wake up alone. It was 7:15. Beau and Tyler would be home any minute and it would have been a bit embarrassing if Jodie hadn't woken up before they got there. He got out of bed and pulled on his pants. Maybe the four of them could order in a pizza or something. And maybe the boys would turn in at a decent hour so he and Jodie could sneak back to bed and spend the night together.

Damn, but he was going to miss her when she was gone.

He picked up his cell and turned it on, surprised there were no messages from clients. Apparently the Fates had been with him.

"Jodie," he called as he walked into the dark living room. He snapped on a light. "Jodie?" he repeated, getting an odd sensation in the pit of his stomach.

The house was empty. Dark and empty.

He turned on the kitchen light as he entered the room, then went to the coat rack and grabbed his jacket. He jogged across the lawn separating the house from the clinic. His truck was there, the Spitfire was not.

She was gone.

Where? Why?

Sam stood for a moment, looking at the empty spot

where the slick little car had been parked up until about an hour ago, judging from the tracks. Big fat snowflakes were falling, and there was maybe a quarter inch of snow covering her tire marks. She hadn't been gone long. Maybe she was just going for takeout for them? Or she wanted to show up after the boys got home, so it wouldn't appear as if they had spent the day together in bed?

Or maybe Sam was clutching at straws. If she'd done any of those things, she would have woken him first. Told him.

She was gone.

Why?

The Beast roared into the drive a few minutes after Sam had returned to the house and attempted unsuccessfully to call Jodie. Twice. He was pacing through the kitchen, trying to make sense of the situation, when the boys burst in, jubilant because the booster club had come up with the funds to send the team to the state tournament in Reno a day early so that they could be well rested.

"Great," Sam said, attempting a hearty response, when at the moment he really didn't care about basketball.

"Yeah," Tyler said. "We're leaving right after school tomorrow. We have to do laundry tonight and pack."

"What's wrong?" Beau demanded.

Sam frowned at him. "Nothing."

Beau gave him a long "yeah, right" look and Sam caved, knowing he had to tell them something.

"Jodie had to go back to Las Vegas. I'm just worried about her on these roads." And wondering where the hell she was and why she'd left like she did.

Beau's expression cleared. "You'll probably go see her sometime, right?"

"I imagine," Sam said vaguely. "I have to go check the messages in the clinic." He grabbed the keys off the hook and went out into the night without a jacket, hitting Redial on the phone as he walked across the lawn.

Nothing.

The gnawing sensation in his gut was almost making him nauseous. What in the hell was going on?

It was after nine when Sam called Margarite. The housekeeper sounded perplexed when she said hello. Apparently she didn't get that many personal calls.

"It's Sam. Do you know where Jodie is?"

"On her way to Las Vegas."

"When did she leave?"

"Just before noon. She had a fight with Joe and left."

Great. So as far as her family knew, she'd been on the road to Vegas when she'd actually been making love to him.

"So she hasn't called to say she's there?"

"Not that I know of, but Nadine has been holed up in her bedroom since Jodie left. It's not the happiest of times here, Sam."

"I can imagine." He ran a hand over the stiff muscles at the back of his neck. "Why do *you* stay?" he muttered.

"I like Nadine, and Lucas has a job. Plus it pays well."

"Would you do me a favor?"

"What?"

"Talk to Nadine. See if Jodie got to Vegas all right and call me back."

There was a pause and Sam wondered if Margarite was going to ask why he wasn't in contact with Jodie himself. It didn't take a brainiac, though, to figure out that he'd only be asking if he couldn't contact her, and Margarite was no fool.

"I'll call you as soon as I know something. If you don't hear from me, I don't know anything."

"Thanks." It was all he could ask. Sam paced his office. When Jodie said she was keeping her options open, maybe she meant that she was a free spirit who could come and go as she pleased. Well, she was that. He had no claim on her, but still…

The phone rang, startling him, and he scooped the receiver out of the charger.

"Jodie's at her condo, Sam."

He let out a relieved breath, glad she was home, even if it raised other issues. "Do you have her number there?"

"Just a sec." A moment later Sam had the number. He thanked Margarite and hung up.

Then he programmed the number into his cell and tucked the paper into his personal phone book. She was home. She knew how to get hold of him. Maybe he'd just wait a day and see how this all played out.

Although he still wondered just why he had to do that. This was flipping strange.

IF JODIE'S STOMACH WAS any tighter, it would be inside out. She still felt on the edge of nausea, and after getting home had thrown up.

She'd orphaned the twins, taken Sam's brother from him.

She didn't know how she was going to live the rest of her life knowing that.

Her once a week housekeeper had visited during her absence, so the condo was immaculate. No dust, no sign that it was anything but a showplace, which it was. When Jodie had left Las Vegas eight weeks ago, she'd loved her condo. The minimalist designs and Southwestern color schemes blended beautifully, and the lack of clutter usually soothed Jodie. Today it simply emphasized just how austere her life was. All clean edges. No fraying. No comfort. No fun.

No gym socks on the floor.

She set the grocery bags she carried on the table, then stood for a long moment staring sightlessly across the room.

Sam wouldn't have gym socks on his floor if it hadn't been for her. Those gym socks would have been in the twins' house, and their parents would have been telling the boys to pick them up.

Jodie squeezed her eyes shut and swallowed hard. She was going to have to deal with this. She could call Carmen, tell her she was home early, maybe go out and have a drink….

Her chin dropped to her chest. Jodie wasn't up to seeing any of her friends just yet.

She put the groceries away, lit a few candles to take the staleness out of the air, then settled on the leather sofa to go through the files she'd brought home. Jodie wouldn't go to work for two more days, since she'd left Wesley ahead of schedule, but she'd stopped by the office, anyway. She needed something to distract her and was rewarded by a stack of case files to take home. She sifted through them now to make certain there were no DUIs. No more of those cases for her. Ever.

The phone rang at eight. Jodie didn't move. She let it ring until the machine picked up. And even then she didn't check to see who it was. She'd been in contact with the office. She'd let her mother know she'd arrived home safely. Her father wouldn't be calling anytime soon—not until he was certain Jodie had suffered enough for screwing up. She certainly didn't want to talk to anyone.

Half an hour later the phone rang again. Then fifteen minutes after that.

Jodie gave up and went over to shut the ringer off—which she should have done in the first place—and check the caller identification. She instantly recognized the number.

Sam. Someone had given him her home number. Well, it sure as heck hadn't been her father. She pressed her lips together, and then after a brief hesitation, turned the phone off.

JODIE DID NOT TURN ON either phone on for two days. Her cell phone sat in the bottom of her purse, in case of emergencies, and she ignored her land line. She figured if Sam kept calling and she didn't answer, he'd get the message. It was fun while it lasted, but the city girl had gone back to her bright lights.

She was being cowardly, but right now she'd much rather have him despise her for being shallow than know the truth.

"Are you all right?" Penelope, the receptionist, asked when Jodie came in on Thursday dressed for a brief court appearance in a navy suit that made her look paler than usual. There was nothing wrong with the suit, but there was plenty wrong with her. Apparently, having only one or two hours of sleep a night was beginning to show. She'd put on blush that morning, but had ended up with two pink patches on unnaturally pale skin, so had washed it off again, going for the wan look.

People didn't want wan lawyers. She was going to have to stop on the way home and pick up some bronzer. And more concealer for the circles under her eyes.

"I think I'm coming down with a cold."

"You sure look like it." Penelope had never been known for her tact, and Jodie suspected the only reason she was at the front desk was because she had something on one of the partners. She was a bombshell in the classic tradition, possibly an ex-showgirl, so Jodie could see it happening. "Why don't you take some time off?"

"I've already taken time off," Jodie reminded her. Kicking around alone in her condo was killing her, but she couldn't bring herself to call Carmen, who would lecture her. She didn't feel close enough to any of her other friends to confess what she'd done. And she didn't feel like going out and pretending to have fun when she wasn't.

How had that happened? How had she ended up with acquaintances rather than friends? Those eighty-hour weeks, probably. Who had time for friends? Or a husband, for that matter?

But now she welcomed the work. Anything to take her mind off…

Yeah.

As if anything could.

CHAPTER FOURTEEN

JODIE WAS READING OVER a brief when her doorbell sounded at ten o'clock Saturday morning. She'd been up since dawn, but hadn't done anything except read. The jacket she'd worn the day before was tossed carelessly over the back of an ebony dining room chair, and her briefcase was lying open on a coffee table cluttered with unread mail.

She padded across the carpet in her bare feet, wondering who the heck would be at her door without calling first, then remembered no one could call first. Her brain was going. She looked through the peephole and felt the blood drain from her face. No. Make that her entire body.

Sam.

She stepped back and stared at the door, running through options in her head. Pretty simple. Open the door or leave it closed.

The doorbell rang again. And again. Then he started knocking. Next thing, the neighbors would be complaining, and she'd be talking to the condo board.

Get it over with.

She unlocked the door and pulled it open, letting her hand drop from the carved brass knob as she took a step backward. For a moment she and Sam simply stared at one another, and it wasn't too hard to figure out that he was pissed off in a royal way.

"Why didn't you answer my calls?" he asked without stepping inside.

"Come in," Jodie said, moving back another few feet.

"Why?" he repeated, not budging.

"Damn it, get in here," she said.

He took three steps forward, just enough so that Jodie could close the door behind him.

"I don't understand what happened," he said.

"I know," she replied matter-of-factly.

"Then why don't you fill me in?"

"There's something you don't know about me." Jodie glanced away momentarily. "Something bad."

"How bad can it be?" Sam asked, in a surprisingly gentle voice that made Jodie feel rotten for having strung him along as she had. Damn, but she'd done a number on him.

She squared her shoulders. "I defended Colin Craig. I'm the one who got him off for his third DUI. He would have gone to prison if I hadn't done that."

The expressions that crossed Sam's face were easy to read, because Jodie had felt every one of them herself multiple times since learning the truth. Shock, anger, incredulity. Pain. Lots of pain. Only her pain had come slowly, amplifying as she'd fallen for Sam.

"How long have you known?"

She forced herself to meet his eyes. "For a long time,"

she whispered, preparing herself for what had to come next. "Before we made love. I've essentially been lying to you for weeks now."

Sam stared blindly across the room. Jodie's fingers started to ache and she realized she had a death grip on the back of the ebony chair she'd tossed her jacket onto earlier. She let go and crossed her arms in front of her, hugging herself.

"At least I understand why you left." He turned back to her, his face pale. "I need to think about this."

"What's to think about, Sam?"

"Will you let me in when I come back?"

"Don't come back, Sam."

"Will you let me in?" he asked again.

Jodie's shoulders rose and fell as she inhaled, exhaled, wished there was some way out of this. "I don't know how you got into the complex in the first place," she said numbly.

"I walked through the gate when a car drove through. Your security sucks."

"The gate code is the last four digits of my phone number. And yes...I'll let you in."

It was the least she could do. Let him rage at her before he disappeared from her life.

It was soon obvious that Sam didn't need the gate code. He never left the complex. For over an hour he sat on a chair in the courtyard under the palms and simply stared into the distance, while Jodie occasionally went to her window and stared at him.

She wanted more than anything to make him stop hurting.

She couldn't.

When Sam finally stood, she figured the odds were fifty-fifty as to whether he'd go back out through the gate or come up to her condo. He started for her building and Jodie's heart sank.

Well, at least it would all be over soon.

She went to wait by the door. Sam only had to ring the bell once before she opened it and stepped back to let him in.

The verdict wasn't at all what she expected. Instead of cold anger, Sam simply said, "You should have told me what happened."

"In hindsight, I can see that," she answered coolly. "I was selfish." Incredibly, monumentally selfish.

"We could have faced this together. Talked about it."

Jodie stared at him, stunned. "Talked about it?" she asked incredulously. "Are you crazy? I pretty much killed your brother."

Anger flashed across Sam's face. "Did you hold the bottle to Craig's lips? Put the car keys in his hands?"

"I made sure he was in a position to do just that."

Sam inhaled deeply. "You know what really bugs me?"

"I slept with you?"

"That you have so little faith in me."

"What?" Not the answer she expected. What did faith in him have to do with anything?

"Yeah. You could have told me," he reiterated. "Granted, we'd only been together for a while, but..."

His mouth tightened as the words trailed off. "I thought we had the beginning of something that could grow strong."

"And then things changed," Jodie said bitterly. She felt the sting of tears and turned her head away so she wasn't looking at him. "You cannot have a relationship with someone who killed your brother."

"Stop saying that!"

"And stop being so damned noble. No matter how forgiving you might be now, don't you think this is going to matter just a wee bit in the future? Don't you think Tyler and Beau are pretty much going to hate me when they find out?"

"It won't be easy," Sam agreed.

"It would be impossible. I know."

"How?"

"Just trust me. I know."

"Damn it, Jodie." He crossed the space between them and took hold of her shoulders. Jodie winced, from guilt rather than pain, and he instantly released her.

"We could at least make an attempt to work this out instead of just abandoning all possibilities."

"Sam," she said wearily, "think about what you're saying."

"Jodie—"

"Bottom line, Sam. I won't do this to your nephews. I won't do it to you. We are no more."

"Tell me one thing."

Her belly tightened at his tone. She knew what was coming. "What?"

"Did you feel like you were falling in love with me? Before?"

She still felt as if she was falling in love with him, which made the situation that much worse. "It doesn't matter."

She'd expected him to demand an actual answer, as her father would have. He didn't.

Instead, he crossed to the door. "Would you consider answering my calls in the future?"

She hugged her arms around her even tighter. "No, Sam. That wouldn't be good for any of us." She wasn't taking his calls, she wasn't taking her faher's calls.

His face was pale and his jaw was tight when he turned at the door to give her one last long look. "This isn't over," he said.

Yes. It is.

Sam shut the door behind him. Jodie listened to his footsteps in the hall until she couldn't hear them anymore, then crossed the room and turned the lock.

SAM DROVE HOME, wishing he had another hour or two on the road to figure out how to handle this situation. A big part of him wanted to take the coward's way out and keep Jodie's secret from the boys, because he knew it was going to hurt them. He asked himself over and over again how it would help matters if his nephews knew.

But Paige had told him several times, in several different ways, that shielding the boys wouldn't help them in the long run. So his gut was telling him one thing, the counselor was telling him another. But Tyler and Beau had seemed relieved to finally get to talk about their parents' death.

Okay. Sam was going to come clean and then…hell, he didn't know. He'd figure out some way to clean up this mess. He wasn't ready to let Jodie go.

"How was your trip?" Beau asked, looking up from loading the dishwasher. He straightened when Sam didn't respond as expected. In fact, Sam didn't respond at all.

"What?" Beau asked.

Tyler came into the room carrying a can of air freshener, making Sam wonder briefly just what had gone on in the house while he'd been away. At this point, he didn't care.

"I've got something to tell you."

The brothers, as always, exchanged looks.

"Serious stuff?"

"Yeah."

"But not good serious stuff, right?"

"Not good serious stuff."

"What?" Tyler asked.

"Jodie defended Colin Craig on his third DUI and got him off."

Sam's bald announcement was followed by a moment of frozen silence, and then Beau took the plate in his hand and slammed it down on the counter, his face growing red. "You mean…?"

"I mean that Jodie has connections to the guy."

"No," Tyler said, coming to life. "You mean that she

made it possible for that guy to kill our parents." He stood with the air freshener can in one hand, gripping it so tightly his fingers were turning white. "Shit!"

There had been no way to sugarcoat the situation. No way to tell them that their trail of logic was flawed, because Tyler had a point.

Beau put his hands on the counter and stood with his head bent while Tyler glared at Sam as if this was his fault.

"I liked her," Tyler growled. "I liked her and..."

Beau kept mumbling the same foul word over and over again, staring down at the counter between his hands. Tyler turned and walked out of the room. A second later the bedroom door slammed shut.

Beau looked up at Sam, blinking back tears. "I don't want to see her anymore." He started out of the kitchen. "Ever," he added as he disappeared into the hall. The bedroom door opened and shut again, this time with a quiet click that sounded worse than the slam.

Sam closed his eyes for a moment. How in hell was he supposed to handle this?

Give them time. Let them have their anger. He could hear Paige's patient voice in his head.

Fine. He'd do that. In the meantime his gut was twisted so tightly he felt he was going to puke.

TWO DAYS LATER Sam was nearly worn down by his nephews' anger. They felt betrayed, and because of that they were fixating on Jodie's part in their parents' deaths.

Sam had a blessedly full workload, and when he wasn't pulling a calf or treating scours, he was busy in the office. Katie had taken the week off because her sister in Montana had a baby, so he was on his own. He didn't mind. It kept his thoughts occupied so he couldn't dwell on the reality of the crappy situation he was in.

Until he went to bed. Then he lay awake staring up at the ceiling and wishing that he hadn't connected with Jodie quite so well. Wishing he hadn't fallen in love with her. Wishing she trusted him enough to work through this with him, maybe see Paige at some point in the future, maybe give him a chance to work a miracle.

Maybe if Mike hadn't quit, and she'd continued to show him the lawyer facade, everything would have turned out differently. But it hadn't. He'd gotten to know the real Jodie and he'd fallen for her. Now he had a problem, because he wasn't going to let her slip through his fingers without a fight.

"So what do you think, Dave?" he asked his brother out loud. He'd developed the habit of talking to Dave during the weeks following his death. It had helped him work out the pain and anger, helped him stay strong for his nephews. Dave had been silent over the past several weeks, though. Sam had no idea what his brother would have thought of this turn of events.

He did know instinctively that Dave would have wanted his sons to heal. But how?

The obvious answer was by letting go of the anger. But again, how? Especially when the twins were barely speaking to him. They were angry at him, angry at Jodie.

Sam needed to talk to Paige, who was, unfortunately, on a two-week vacation. Funny how long they'd survived without her, and now her input seemed essential.

WORK DAYS THAT USED TO BE exhausting yet somehow invigorating were now just exhausting. Jodie found no joy in her job, no joy in life, but it was only a phase, she told herself. She'd hoped that being back in the office, away from Sam, would help her regain some perspective. Yes, she was one of many who'd played a part in Dave and Maya Hyatt's deaths, and yes, she'd been doing her job. But she could not move beyond the pain she'd caused two boys she'd come to care for, a man she'd quite possibly fallen in love with. Or the pain she might inadvertently cause others if she made the same mistake again.

A DUI case had come her way, a slam dunk, but she'd turned it down, causing much gossip and a few back handsprings from the junior associate who'd ended up with the case. Jodie was not going there again.

She wasn't going anywhere. It was obvious that the partners were concerned about her lackluster attitude since returning, so she'd confessed what had happened to the senior.

He'd nodded sagely, then told her to get her ass in gear and grind out some cases. Which was what she was doing now. At home, at work.

Damn, but she was tired.

She was asleep when the phone rang. A quick glance at the wall clock told her it was ten o'clock—too early to go to bed, and too late for Sam to be calling. But he was. Jodie hesitated, then pushed the button to receive the call.

Her voice was husky from sleep when she said hello.

"You picked up." It was almost physically painful to hear his voice.

"Yes."

"You didn't when I called before."

"I'd forgotten my phone at home." Jodie pressed her fingertips to her forehead and closed her eyes. She wished she didn't feel so strongly for this guy. "So how's everything there?" Banal words considering the circumstances.

She heard Sam inhale. "Some things are good. Others…"

"Tyler and Beau?"

"Their team took second place in state. Beau was leading scorer."

"Tell him congratula—" Jodie stopped abruptly. "Do they know, Sam? Did you tell them?"

"Yeah."

It was her turn to inhale deeply. "How'd they take it?"

"Not too well."

"I told you," she said softly.

"They'll deal with it."

She continued to massage her forehead, staving off the tension headache building there. "Tell me this…are they angry with me?"

"Yes, but—"

"Don't tell me they'll get over it."

"*You* need to get over it, Jodie! The judge and the cops made it possible, too. The bartender made it possible. The man who sold the asshole the car made it possible."

"I know that. But none of those guys are in a position to be part of your nephew's lives, are they?" she asked reasonably. "Let this go, Sam. It'll be easier on everyone in the long run."

She moved the phone away from her ear and pushed the off button.

ONE MORE WEEK UNTIL Paige returned. Sam hoped he could hold it together for that long. Tyler and Beau were hanging on to their anger, and between the two of them, nurturing it. Not what he had expected when he'd told them the truth.

Finally Sam had had it. After a silent dinner, Tyler started clearing the table, but Sam told him to stop.

"We're going to discuss this."

"There's nothing to discuss," Beau said, echoing words Sam had said to him more than once. "Jodie gets people off so they can go out and do the same thing all over again."

"She was just doing her job. It's the way the law works. The judge and the cops that screwed up the procedure are to blame, too. It was circumstances."

"Well, it sucks."

"Yeah, it does."

"So pretty much everybody else is to blame for Mom and Dad getting hit by that car except for Jodie?" Beau asked in a challenging tone.

"That's not what I said."

Ty shook his head and walked out of the room. Beau gave his uncle a long look and then followed his brother.

Sam leaned his hands on the counter and let his head drop. In Tyler's own words, this sucked.

Things weren't any better with Jodie. He'd tried again to call her and, just as before, she refused to pick up his calls. He thought briefly about using another phone, then decided not to use those tactics. She needed time, the boys needed time. The problem was that time didn't seem to be making anyone heal. It simply seemed to exacerbate the situation.

Finally, he realized he couldn't wait for Paige to get back. He needed some moral support. Now. He got her cell number from Tricia and called, thankful that Paige did not seem to mind him hunting her down and impinging on her private time.

He told her what had happened, how he'd handled it. It was so weird to be doing this. A few months ago, before he'd called Tricia at the high school, he never would have poured out his personal life to anyone. But now he was desperate. He wanted to save his nephews, and he wanted a chance with Jodie.

Paige was silent for a moment, then said, "Sam… you've given them a scapegoat. Someone they can blame other than Colin Craig."

"Did I make a mistake?"

"No, but just because you were up front doesn't mean the people involved are going to see things the way you do."

"Is there any hope?"

"I wish I knew," she said softly. "My advice is to keep the doors of communication open. Allow the boys time to deal with the anger."

"What if they never deal with it?"

"You mean what if they never accept Jodie again?"

Sam put a hand to his forehead. "Yeah. That's exactly what I mean."

"It may happen, Sam. I'm sorry. But regardless of that—"

"I need to step back and let them deal with this."

"I'm afraid you do. But...maybe I could talk to the boys? Give them something to do until I get back and we can meet again in person?"

"That'd be good." *And do something miraculous while you're at it.* He went down the hall to the boys' bedroom and tapped on the door.

"Yeah?" Tyler's sullen voice came through the closed panel.

"Paige wants to talk to you guys. She's on the phone."

The door opened, and first Beau came out and then Tyler. They silently walked past him and down the hall to the office as if they were going to the gallows. But Paige must have done some good, because the call took almost a half hour, during which time Sam did the dishes and started a load of laundry.

When it ended, Beau and Tyler came back into the kitchen.

"We're going to meet with her alone next week," Beau said, before heading down the hall.

Tyler was more forthcoming. "She gave us some stuff to work on."

"All right," Sam said, hoping for more information.

"This is kinda harder on Beau than it is on me, Sam. He really liked Jodie a lot."

"I know."

Tyler tightened his mouth, as if to keep from saying anything more. He nodded at Sam and then followed his brother down the hall.

CHAPTER FIFTEEN

"YOU GOT A LETTER," Penelope said as Jodie walked by. She handed her a plain white envelope addressed by hand to Jodie in care of the law office. "Be careful of anthrax," she said as she looked back at her keyboard.

"Thanks," Jodie muttered, tearing the envelope open as she walked. But she waited until she was in her office before pulling out the single sheet of computer paper. The postmark said Wesley, NV, and the writing was not Sam's. Jodie had a very bad feeling about this.

She shut her door, hung up her jacket, booted up her computer. Only then did she unfold the letter, which she'd set on her desk, and start to read. By the time she'd finished, she was numb, yet oddly grateful.

Beau Hyatt pulled no punches. He hated her. He never wanted to see her again. He wished something bad would happen in her life so she could feel real pain.

Jodie set the open letter on her desk and leaned back in her chair, regarding it dispassionately.

What more evidence did Sam need that there was no future for the two of them?

She folded the paper and slid it back into the envelope, then put it in her briefcase for safekeeping. As time passed and she started to feel hopeful, she would pull it out and read it.

Perhaps she'd even read it again tonight. For penance.

During the days following the letter, Jodie was even more off her game than she'd been before, making stupid mistakes—or rather, overlooking things that had never escaped her in the past.

She put her head down on her desk after realizing that she'd missed an important point in the case she was preparing. Damn Sam and damn her father. Most of all damn Colin Craig.

Sam had tried to call several times after returning to Wesley. Her father hadn't tried to call her once. Magnanimous forgiveness put a person in the same position as withholding love did. The bottom slot. Jodie hated being there, hated being the one who owed something to someone else.

The brief she was resting her head on was warm beneath her cheek, fresh out of an overworked copy machine. She closed her eyes. Tried to count her blessings.

She had her health.

One corner of her mouth quirked sardonically and she raised her head, sat back in her chair.

She had a job that she'd found challenging up until a few weeks ago. Now she felt as if she was barely able to focus on it. The work that had gotten her through her divorce wasn't helping her out now. In fact…it was hard to admit…she was beginning to feel overwhelmed. And her boss had been none too pleased when she refused the DUI case he'd assigned her.

She was edging closer and closer to hating her job.

She had to do something. Did she want to give up the law? No. But—and a few months ago she never would have believed she would be thinking this way—she wanted less pressure. Fewer hours.

She didn't want to be in a position where she might be making life-and-death decisions by putting people out on the street again who shouldn't be there. She was spending so much time second-guessing herself that she was no longer effective in her job.

She dropped her head back into her hands. She was going to become a freaking real estate attorney if she kept acting this way.

Jodie went shopping on her way home, picking up supplies for her nearly empty fridge. Driving out of the parking lot, she almost hit a car because she wasn't focused.

She went home, made a fried egg sandwich and started reviewing career options. Maybe a smaller town, a smaller firm. Nothing as small as Wesley, but maybe a city with fewer DUIs, fewer people than Vegas. Maybe somewhere in Montana. She'd grown up in Illinois and was used to the cold. After her weeks on the ranch, she kind of missed the rural life, although she'd rather be in a small town than miles away from one. It wasn't likely she'd be spending time on her father's ranch in the foreseeable future. Even if he did loosen up and deign to forgive her, for once in her life, Jodie wasn't certain she was going to return the favor. She'd had it with yo-yo affection. Better to just cut bait.

Her only concern was her mother, whom she talked to a couple times a week. Nadine never said a word about Joe, and Jodie never fessed up about Sam. Instead they talked about painting, Jodie's job, cooking. Ultimately, Jodie decided that she and her mother could continue their relationship as they had up until now—by meeting in a city and spending the weekend together, with Joe out of the loop. Sad, but realistic.

She paced through the house. So did she seriously start planning a change? Or wait and see if this was a phase, caused by an unexpected trip into a Sam Hyatt-inspired fantasyland, which ended as all fantasies must—crushed by a heavy dose of reality? Jodie had never been a big believer in happily ever after. All she had to do was look at her parents' marriage to know that no matter how much in love you might be, one partner always seemed to be on the losing end.

So bottom line—she needed to regroup, get back on top of her game. And yes, it might be with another firm, in another city, but for right now she was going to do the best she could with the job she had. After all, she was Jodie Barton De Vanti. This was what she did best.

THE BELLS ON THE CLINIC door rang a few minutes after Katie had left for the day, and Sam assumed she'd forgotten her keys. But the footsteps that came into the office were heavy, booted.

Sam pushed back his chair and got up. The last person he expected to see standing next to his counter was Joe Barton.

"I have a question for you." Joe did not look good. His face was drawn, the lines in it more apparent than they'd been the last time Sam had seen him, at the feed store a week ago.

"What's that?" Sam asked, meeting the older man's gaze dead-on.

"Do you have anything to do with Jodie not returning my calls?"

Sam couldn't hold back the disbelieving snort. "I think that's all you, Joe."

Not what he'd wanted to hear. His thick black brows drew closer together. "I heard you two were… involved."

"It's none of your business if we were."

"Damn it!" Joe exclaimed angrily. "I want to know if that's why she won't talk to me!"

"No!" Sam shouted back. He ran a hand over the side of his head, telling himself to cool it. A yelling match in the clinic wouldn't do either of them any good, and shouting was Joe's modus operandi. Be scarier than the guy coming at you. Then he'll back off. Sam had known other people like Joe and refused to play that game.

"I don't believe you."

"So what do you think I did? Poisoned her mind against you?"

Joe didn't answer, probably because the accusation did sound stupid when spoken out loud.

"It likely has something to do with you yelling at her for calling me out to your place."

"I've yelled at her before."

"Maybe she's had enough."

A shadow crossed Joe's features, as if he'd wondered that himself. "She's never done this before."

"She's thirty years old. Maybe she's tired of being a good girl, tired of trying to live up to your demands for perfection."

"What the hell are you talking about?"

Sam gave Joe a withering look. "What do you think I'm talking about?"

"I never demanded perfection."

"That's not what I heard."

Joe looked surprised, so surprised that he forgot to appear intimidating, and for a brief second Sam was treated to a glimpse of a confused and concerned old man. "Explain what you mean."

"She's tired of you demanding that she be the best in everything. She's tired of having to live her life without making mistakes."

"What in the hell are you talking about? I never told her she had to be the best, that she couldn't make mistakes. I wanted her to do the best she was capable of."

"That wasn't what she heard," Sam replied flatly.

Joe ran a hand over the lower part of his face, then gave Sam a lawyerlike glare. "Are you being truthful? Or just trying to get back at me for suing you?"

"If I'd wanted to do that, your gelding would have bled to death in the snow and you'd be short about five healthy calves."

Joe planted his hands on his hips, glanced down at the floor, then back up at Sam. He shook his head and walked out of the clinic without another word.

Sam watched him go, feeling both anger at the man's arrogance and stubbornness, and a twinge of empathy because he now had an idea of just how damned hard it was to raise a kid, how many mistakes there were to make. It seemed as if Joe had made his share, too.

Sam went to his desk, sat in the chair and leaned back. He didn't doubt for one moment that Joe had wanted Jodie to be the best, but his trip here must have cost him his pride. He'd come to ask what the deal was from the guy he despised most in this town. Yeah, that had to be tough.

It didn't make Sam like the guy any more, but he could better understand Jodie's relationship with her father.

And perhaps why she was doing what she was.

Jodie thought love was conditional. Screw up and love was gone. That was how Joe had motivated her to be the best. Affection for the winner, a cold shoulder for the loser.

Successfully defending Colin Craig had made Jodie a loser. She'd been truthful when she said she expected no forgiveness. She hadn't had a lot of that in her life. Instead of forgiveness, she'd won back affection by achieving.

Good thing Joe had left, because Sam was feeling a strong urge to throttle the man.

THE BOYS CAME HOME after school, since there was no basketball practice.

"I want to talk to you guys. About Jodie," Sam announced. Their expressions instantly changed.

"What about her?" Tyler asked.

"I care about her. A lot."

Tyler stared at him. "That's cool, Sam. Really cool." He spoke with no warmth in his voice.

Sam's control snapped. "People make mistakes, you guys!" He had certainly made his share and he was probably making one now, but he didn't care. It couldn't mess up the situation any more than it was now. "I make them. You make them. Jodie makes them. She didn't kill your parents any more than I did when I talked your dad into taking my place at the conference, so I'm to blame, too. She's just an easy target because she doesn't put food on your table and a roof over your head."

Tyler swallowed, but didn't look away. Beau was staring at the floor.

"She can't make what happened to you right," Sam continued in a gentler voice. "No one can."

The boys gave no response, but he hadn't expected one.

"I want you guys to think about what your parents would want you to do in this situation."

That got their attention.

"Do you think they'd be happy knowing you two

were determined to hang on to the anger and let it eat you from the inside out? That you were generating hate on their account?"

Beau shifted his weight, propping a hand on one hip, and Tyler continued his critical stare, but other than that, both remained disengaged. No more than Sam expected, but he had to give it a shot, hope that someday his words might make sense. That obviously wasn't today.

"That's all," he said in defeat. "I have a call. I won't be home until late. Do your homework."

He grabbed the keys off the peg and let himself out the back door, crossing the lawn to the clinic with long strides, not thinking about what he'd just said, because frankly, he didn't believe it would do much good. The boys were taking comfort in their anger and they now had someone tangible to direct it at, rather than some faceless guy in prison. Or maybe they just felt betrayed, because like him, they'd fallen in love with Jodie. The only difference was that he still loved her and didn't know what to do about it.

Sam ended up spending a good chunk of the night at Kade Danning's place, trying to save a horse that a pack of dogs had made run through a wire fence. Kade's wife, Libby, whom Sam had once dated, was furious, since she'd made complaints to the authorities about the owner several times and nothing was done. Now one of their mares was a bloody, stitched up mess. But she would pull through.

As Sam worked he couldn't help reliving the night he'd broken his vow to himself and gone to the Barton ranch to sew up Joe's gelding for Jodie. He'd had no idea what a life-altering event that would turn out to be, and now he wondered how it was all going to play out.

It was beginning to look less than hopeful.

Kade and Libby offered Sam a bed when he'd finished stitching, since it was after midnight, but he declined the offer. It was only an hour back to Wesley, after all.

He could barely stay awake. It seemed the nights he was able to sleep were interrupted by emergencies, and the nights he didn't have calls he lay awake, his gut tied in a knot.

Something had to give.

The next morning he felt like crap. His head was pounding and he couldn't seem to get enough coffee in him, so of course the call from hell came in.

"Sam, it's the Barton ranch." There was something in Katie's voice that kept Sam from telling her he wasn't available. "Margarite."

He took the phone and gave a curt hello.

"Sam, Joe just had a heart attack pulling a calf. The ambulance should be here any minute.... Sam, that poor cow is going to die and Lucas can't finish the job. And we have two more cows down."

"Be right there."

Katie was wide-eyed when Sam handed the phone back to her. "Joe's had a heart attack. I need to go help."

"With the heart attack?" Katie asked in a bewildered voice.

"With the cows. He was pulling a calf when it happened and two more are about to give birth."

He was out the door before the last words left his mouth. He might think Joe Barton was a son of a bitch, but he didn't want him to die, didn't want Jodie to go through the anguish of losing him while they still had unfinished business.

The Beast pulled in just as Sam was getting into his truck.

"What's up?" Beau asked.

"Joe Barton just had a heart attack."

"Is he alive?" Tyler asked.

"Yeah."

Beau snorted. "Too bad Jodie won't find out what it's like to lose a dad," he muttered darkly.

Sam's hand froze on the door handle, then he slowly turned back to face his nephews. Beau swallowed when he saw his expression.

"Is that what you want? Really? You want Jodie to feel what you felt? If so, then I feel sorry for *you*."

Beau's color started to rise.

"Tell you what, bud. You can hold on to your bitterness for as long as you want. I don't care. I'm done, because nothing makes a difference. But do not ever spout that shit around me again. Got it?"

After a stretch of heavy silence, both teens nodded, then Beau looked down at the ground, scuffing the toe of one sneaker on the ground self-consciously.

"And you know what? Your dad would be damned embarrassed right now. He raised you guys better than this."

Sam didn't say another word. He got into the truck, started it and backed out of the driveway, leaving his nephews staring after him.

He saw the ambulance approaching him on the road leading from the Barton ranch, its red lights flashing. Sam pulled over, thinking that the lights were a good sign. The medics didn't bother when it was too late. Right behind the ambulance was a fancy sedan, with Margarite at the wheel and Nadine Barton sitting beside her.

Was Jodie on her way up north right now? Had they called her? Or were they waiting until they had more news?

Lucas was in the barn. He shook his head when Sam approached.

"You lost the cow?" Sam asked.

"Yeah. It just took too long." He indicated the two cows in separate pens, both down. "She's probably going to be fine, but that one's a heifer and Joe used that big bull."

Damn Joe and that black homozygous bull of his. "Well, let's see what we can do to help her out."

After a brief examination, Sam knew he was looking at a C-section. They put the heifer in the squeeze and Sam started shaving the left flank.

"Are you staying on?" he asked Lucas, making a stab at normal conversation.

"I guess. Me and Joe seem to be doing all right."

"Glad to hear it. Is he hiring more help?"

"The usual summer hires for when he turns the place into a glorified dude ranch, but nothing right now.

Calving is keeping me busy. I wish I had more time for the fences now that the snow's melting. They're sagging bad and I'm afraid we'll have an escape before I get them all tightened."

"Who's been doing the vet work?"

"Eriksson when he has time to come. Pretty much Joe's been helping me pull the calves, and other than one C-section that Dr. E did, we've been lucky." Lucas handed Sam the Bentadine and Sam swabbed the area of the incision before handing it back. "That black bull? Died of red water. Eriksson did a swab to make sure."

"How'd Joe take that?" Sam checked the rafters for pulleys in case they had to draw the calf out of the incision with chains.

"Joe's been pretty darned quiet about that."

"I wonder if he apologized to Jodie."

Lucas snorted. "I haven't seen any flying pigs lately." He was quiet for a moment while Sam readied himself to make the incision. "I kind of wonder if worrying about Jodie didn't...you know...lead up to the heart attack."

"Straining on a calf probably didn't do him any good, either."

"Self-loathing's a bad thing," Lucas replied, sounding as if he was talking from experience. "If Joe lives through this, I hope he figures that out. Makes some things right."

"Yeah," Sam said as he began his operation. "Me, too."

CHAPTER SIXTEEN

WHEN SAM GOT HOME, the boys were gone.

He was getting so damned tired of this stomach-in-a-knot feeling. Was anything in his life ever going to go smoothly again? The only positive thing was that Margarite told him Joe had been stabilized and Jodie was on her way to the hospital.

Sam walked through the empty house, looking for clues, such as a note, before he dialed the twins' cell and heard it ringing in their bedroom. Cool. He snapped his own phone shut and went to find theirs, lying on the dresser next to Beau's wallet. Okay, wherever they went, they weren't going to spend a lot of money. Although Beau was not the greatest at math, he was the brother who managed his money best and had the most. Tyler was always broke.

Sam looked down at the phone, then shook his head. He'd have to see about getting them each a line instead of making them share. A year ago he'd figured it was a waste of money since the brothers were usually together, but now it didn't seem like such a bad idea.

He sat on Tyler's bed, which was as neat as Beau's was rumpled, closed his eyes, breathed in and out. In and out. He and his nephews had not parted under the best of circumstances, and now he was afraid they'd done something stupid out of anger and spite.

He hoped they were stronger than that.

They would be back. He needed to get a grip and go catch up on his office work. If he could focus that long.

IF FLYING TO WESLEY WERE easy, Jodie would have done it, but there was a twice-daily flight into Elko and an hour drive after that. She'd already missed the morning flight when she got the call about her father, so she'd climbed into the Spitfire and started driving. She'd also done the unthinkable—she'd abandoned the cases she was working on. But one of the office vultures would snap them up, and maybe this idea that was playing in her head about moving to another city, working for a smaller firm with less stress, would become a reality, whether she wanted it to or not.

Right now she didn't care. She needed to get to her father before it was too late. The last she'd heard, about an hour out of Vegas, was that the doctors were going to perform bypass surgery. Another hour had passed. Surely no news was good news.

Focus on the road. All her mother needed was another emergency to deal with. Jodie made an effort to slow down to the speed limit. *Focus, focus, focus.*

She was eighty miles from Wesley when her cell phone rang. She was almost afraid to answer it.

"Jodie, it's Margarite. Your mom is with your dad. He made it through all right. He's weak, but...well, he's doing okay."

"I'll be there in an hour," Jodie promised, and then hung up, feeling like a bit of the weight had lifted. But she and her father still had some stuff to work out once he was strong enough. She just hoped it wasn't too late. That she hadn't screwed things up too badly by refusing to talk to him. What if she was the reason he'd had this heart attack?

No. If that was the case, she would have given him one a long time ago. She'd disappointed him enough during her life.

But she'd never before walked out on him.

The Wesley hospital was small, so Jodie was astounded that her father had had his surgery there. Her mother's car was parked in the lot. Margarite was sitting in the waiting room just inside the door.

"Your mom is in with him."

"He's conscious?"

"I don't know. Maybe you better sit down."

"I want to see him."

"The nurse will tell the doctor you're here."

Jodie slowly sat. Margarite reached out and patted her knee. "Does Sam know you're here?"

"No."

"Things are not so good there?" Jodie just shook her head. "That's too bad."

Yes, it was, but short of changing the past, there wasn't much Jodie could do about it.

The big silver door leading to the ICU opened and Jodie's mom came out, accompanied by a doctor wearing green scrubs. A second later Jodie was in her arms.

"It looks like he'll be okay," Nadine said in a teary voice. "There's still the chance of infection and pneumonia, so he has to stay here."

Jodie pulled back, looking down into her mom's face, then up at the doctor who approached them.

"Can I see him?"

"Briefly," the doctor said. "He's probably going to conk out in a few minutes."

Jodie went into the room to find her father surrounded by machines that all seemed to be blipping and beeping. Lying in bed, he looked smaller than before and his color was off. But he opened his eyes when she came close to him and touched his hand. The corners of his mouth tilted up and he managed to give her hand a slight squeeze before his eyes drifted shut again.

"He's going to be out for a while," the surgeon said from behind her.

"I'll wait for him to wake up."

Jodie spent the next several hours with her mother, who insisted on checking into the motel a block away from the hospital.

"It makes more sense than driving back and forth."

"I'll stay there with you."

"Do me a favor," her mother said. "Go back to the ranch and see how your father's cows are doing. I know he'll ask, and an eyewitness report will make him happy. Then pack me a bag for tomorrow and bring it to me. I'll call if there's anything you need to know."

"Couldn't Margarite—"

"She's staying with her sister here in town."

"I don't want to leave you alone."

"Right now…honestly, Jodie, I'd rather be alone."

"Are you sure?"

"Very."

Jodie searched her mother's face and could see she was telling the truth.

"Call if you change your mind. I'll be here in half an hour."

"I know." Nadine hesitated, then stunned Jodie by asking, "Will you see Sam while you're here?"

"No…we've ended our relationship." Jodie looked her in the eye and had the oddest feeling she wasn't fooling her.

"Go get some sleep, hon."

"I will."

Jodie wanted more than anything to ask her mother what to do, how to handle loving a guy she couldn't have. How to live with having done the unforgivable. Instead she left her to her vigil and went out to the parking lot, where she found Sam's vet truck parked next to her car.

Oh. Man.

"Sam…this is not the time," she said, even as she was wishing with all her heart and soul that she could simply walk into his arms. Lean against him and absorb his strength.

"How's your father?" His voice was filled with concern, which didn't help matters.

"He's going to be okay."

"Can I do anything for you or your mom?"

Jodie simply shook her head.

"Stop shutting me out, Jodie."

"What else can I do, since you refuse to take a hint?" she asked, suddenly angry that he was confronting her at a time like this. Didn't she have enough stress? "Why would I go into a situation that's been doomed to heartache from the very beginning?"

"Because we can work through it."

"How many times did you tell me how important it is to you to keep the boys stable? To give them a healing environment?"

"I never said I didn't want them to face challenges."

"Challenges?" Jodie gave a sharp laugh. "Try hate and resentment. Did you see the letter Beau wrote me?"

Sam stilled. "What letter?"

"I'll take that as a no."

"What letter?"

She lifted her chin so she could look him in the eye as she explained. "Beau sent a letter to my law office, telling me exactly how he felt about what I'd done. Your nephew is very articulate."

"When did you get this letter?"

Jodie gestured in frustration. "I don't know. Two weeks ago, maybe? Not long after I got back."

"Things will change."

"They won't change that much," she insisted. People didn't do an about-face. They held grudges and used stuff against you. They jerked you around.

Sam touched her shoulder and she jumped. "Jo..."

His hand didn't move, but stayed there, steady on her shoulder, maintaining a connection. Jodie kept her back stiff.

"Look," she said fiercely. "I'm thinking of the boys and your family."

"And I'm thinking about what a coward you are. The boys are strong enough to work through this. It won't be easy or instantaneous, but I wouldn't say that if I didn't believe it was true."

She shrugged, even though his remark made her furious. "Believe what you will." Then she opened her car and got into the driver's seat.

"People won't stop loving you just because you make a mistake," he said, leaning down to look inside the low-slung vehicle.

"Wanna bet?" Jodie asked through gritted teeth, shoving the key into the ignition.

"I'm not like your dad. You don't have to meet certain conditions to be acceptable."

She gave him a seriously cold look. "Well, aren't you a saint."

"No. I'm a regular guy running out of patience."

"Good," she said, turning the key. "When that happens, maybe you'll come to your senses and do what's right for Beau and Tyler."

YOU DON'T HAVE TO meet certain conditions to be acceptable.

Of course she did. Hadn't she learned that from day one?

The ranch was lit up like a Christmas tree when she

drove up to the garage. The barn lights were on, the house lights were on. When Jodie walked inside, she found the television going and the microwave door hanging open. Her mother and Margarite must have left in one heck of a hurry.

Jodie sat on a kitchen chair and kicked off her ruined shoes. She couldn't believe she'd driven through the snow in a sports car wearing peep-toe pumps and a linen blazer, but when she'd heard about her dad, she'd simply gotten into the Spitfire and driven. She would have been in deep trouble if she'd gotten stuck.

Jodie walked through the house, shutting off lights as she went, and shedding her damp clothing. She tossed her blazer over the back of a teak chair, then unbuttoned her blouse as she walked through the living room. Thankfully, she always kept clothes at the ranch, so she would have something to wear after she got out of the shower. The cold seemed to have seeped inside her bones.

She stood under the hot water until it started to go cold, and she was still chilled. Her dark blue velour robe hung on the back of her bathroom door, right where she'd left it a few weeks ago. She slipped into it, then sat on the bed and pulled on fuzzy socks before padding back through the house to the kitchen to make something hot to eat.

Margarite didn't believe in frozen dinners, but she had the freezer stocked just in case Lucas needed a meal while she was gone. Jodie pulled out macaroni and cheese, peeled back the wrapper and slid it into the microwave, having no clue if she'd even be able to eat it. She'd had nothing since breakfast, and yet didn't feel hungry. Still, a person needed to eat. If nothing else, it would warm her from the inside out.

The timer dinged and Jodie took out the tray, poking at the top before closing the microwave.

Then she heard an odd sound behind her and glanced up to see the reflection of a man in the shiny black microwave door.

Jodie screamed, throwing the plastic plate in the air as she whirled around, her body instinctively going into the defensive stance she'd learned in karate class. The man reacted in almost the same way, shouting and jumping backward, and then Jodie noticed he wasn't exactly a man. Not yet, anyway.

"Beau!"

For a long moment they stared at each other, both wide-eyed, until Beau swallowed hard and Jodie pressed a hand to her heaving chest.

"You. Scared. Me," she said.

"Likewise," Beau muttered, color rising in his cheeks. "I thought Lucas was in here. He said something about getting food. I wanted to tell him we were leaving."

"Why are you *here?*" she asked, still trying to gain control of her breathing and her voice. "At the ranch?"

"We're helping out," Beau said self-consciously.

"Did my dad...hire you?" That made no sense.

Beau snorted. "Right."

"Did Sam send you?"

"He doesn't know we're here."

"Then..."

The boy's gaze shot around the room as if he was looking for an escape route, then came back to her. Briefly. He was even more weirded out than she was by the situation. "Look, I'm sorry I scared you," he said a bit desperately. "But Ty is waiting. I need to leave."

"All right." Jodie couldn't exactly wrestle him down and demand answers, although she was tempted.

"I'll just go out the way I came," he said, jerking his head toward the living room.

She nodded.

"I, uh, I'm sorry about your dad. I hope he's all right."

"He will be," Jodie said numbly.

"Good. Well, bye. Sorry about your supper. Bye."

Beau disappeared back into the living room and a few seconds later Jodie heard the front door open and close.

What about the letter, and why are you here?

And then she automatically grabbed a length of paper towels and bent down to clean up the macaroni.

She hadn't been hungry, anyway.

What in the heck had just happened? Why on earth would Beau be here "helping"? It made no sense. No sense at all.

Let it go. She had other more important issues to think about.

But why would a kid who'd made no secret about the fact that she'd ruined his life come and help out on the ranch?

IT WAS ALMOST SIX O'CLOCK when Tyler and Beau came in through the kitchen door, knocking snow off their boots.

Sam was stirring a pot of soup, having thrown supper together with a can opener, too keyed up to do much else.

"Where've you been?" he asked, hoping he sounded casual. It was dark outside, but not very late, and it wasn't unusual for the boys to be gone all day. Only, for the most part Sam knew exactly where they were, and they hadn't started the day with an emotional confrontation.

"Barton ranch," Tyler said, prying off a boot. Sam almost dropped the spoon.

Beau took his gloves out of his pocket and spread them on the heat register to dry.

"We went to see if Lucas needed some help," Tyler continued. "You had all those calls this afternoon, and we thought…we'd just drive out and see if we could lend a hand, since Joe was in the hospital and all."

"You spent quite a while there," Sam said, not really understanding what had happened.

"Two calves were born and we tightened some fence by hand. We're going back tomorrow. Lucas wants to pay us, but…" Beau glanced down briefly. "After what I said to you about Jodie, and then Joe almost dying… it doesn't really feel right."

Sam nodded. "I bet Lucas appreciated the help."

"He was surprised to see us," Tyler said.

"So was Jodie." Beau pulled off a wet sock and left it on the floor, where it would stay until Sam told him to pick it up later.

"You saw Jodie?"

"I scared the crap out of her. She threw macaroni at me."

Sam frowned, not quite following the macaroni business, but deciding he'd ask about it later. "Why'd you guys go to the ranch in the first place?"

Ty cut a sidelong glance at his brother, who shifted uncomfortably.

"Because I didn't know what else to do," Beau blurted. "I did something I shouldn't have."

"Sent Jodie a letter?"

A stunned look crossed his face. "Yeah."

"How bad was it?"

"Bad," Beau mumbled. Sam didn't say anything, sensing there was more. "Real bad. Mom wouldn't have been too proud of me." He looked everywhere but at Sam for a moment. "Paige told us to write our feelings in a letter to the person we were angry at."

"She told us *not* to mail them," Tyler added grimly.

"I mailed mine," Beau said. "And for about half a day I felt better."

"And then?"

He made an eloquent face. "I tried to tell myself I was right, but it didn't work. So I called Paige after you left today."

"What did she say?" Sam asked quietly.

Beau glanced at his brother as if for encouragement,

then back at Sam. He stood a little taller. "Paige told me that Jodie didn't know that guy was going to…kill someone. Nobody could have known that."

Sam wanted to ask the kid how many times he'd heard that exact same sentiment from his uncle, but managed to hold the words in as Beau started talking again. "And she told me I had to forgive Jodie, and I had to forgive myself for being an asshole and sending the letter, or I was never going to be whole again."

Tears started forming in Beau's eyes. He looked up at the ceiling to hold them back before saying in an unsteady voice, "I really kinda want to be whole again."

Sam couldn't wait any longer. He reached out and pulled Beau into a rough embrace, realizing that the kid had grown—he was taller than the last time Sam had done this, only a month ago.

After an awkward pause, Tyler stepped forward to put his arms around both of them. "Don't want to miss the group hug," he muttered, but Sam had a feeling that the kid actually meant it.

CHAPTER SEVENTEEN

JODIE PACED THE ranch house after checking in with Lucas to see what the deal was with the boys. Apparently they'd showed up and offered to help, so he'd gratefully put them to work. They were coming back the next day.

She didn't get it. Not after the letter Beau had written. People didn't just do one-eighties like that.

She stopped pacing in the kitchen and leaned her forehead against the cool glass of the picture window.

Why were Sam's nephews paying penance, when she was the one who'd committed the crime?

Let it go.

She couldn't. She wanted answers and she wanted them now.

Jodie packed a bag for her mother and one for herself, since she'd be spending the night in town, in the motel. She wasn't driving back to the ranch twice, but she *was* going to talk to Sam. She intended to get answers, set boundaries. She did not want his nephews at the ranch, reminding her of the mistake she'd unwittingly made.

She got into the Spitfire with every intention of settling the situation once and for all. Unfortunately, she wasn't going to get the chance. Both the clinic and the house were dark and the vet truck was gone when she arrived. The Hyatt men must have gone on a call and she was not going to get any answers tonight.

As she entered the hospital, Jodie hid her disappointment at not being able to hash things out with Sam behind her lawyer face. Her mother was on her feet the instant she saw her.

"What's wrong? Why are you here?"

So much for hiding things. "I couldn't stay at that ranch alone. I brought your stuff. How's Dad?"

"He's sleeping." Nadine sounded determined to remain positive. "We can see him first thing in the morning."

Jodie put her arm around her mother's thin shoulders. "Why don't we go to the motel? Get some sleep in a real bed so we can make it through tomorrow without being all tired and cranky?"

Nadine smiled slightly, since she'd always cajoled Jodie into bed by telling her she didn't want her to be tired and cranky the next day.

"All right." Nadine gathered her magazines and needlework, carefully arranging them in a Gucci tote before putting on her coat. "And once we get to the motel, you can tell me what's going on with you and this vet."

Jodie gave her a sidelong glance. "I already told you—"

"He's called twice today to check on your father. The nurses told me. I want to know the whole story."

Nadine had already checked into the motel, so it wasn't long before she had her daughter seated in the rather uncomfortable upholstered chair next to the desk, while she sat on the edge of the bed. Once again she asked for the entire story.

Jodie gave her the bare bones—she and Sam had had a fling, she'd made the startling discovery that she'd defended the man who'd killed his brother, his nephews hated her and one of them had sent her a letter saying that very clearly. Oh, and Sam was trying to hold his family together, and having her around wasn't helping matters.

"Anything else?" Nadine asked in a shrewd voice. She would have made a good interrogator, Jodie decided. Not because she was intimidating, but because she could read body language.

"The boys were at the ranch when I got there. Helping Lucas."

"Why?"

"I have no idea," Jodie said wearily. "I wanted to ask Sam, but his truck wasn't at his place. He must be out on a call. And…now that I think about it, Beau said Sam didn't know they were there."

"But you went to him, anyway."

Jodie gave her mother a sharp look. "I wanted answers."

"I can give you some answers. It sounds like the boys are trying to make amends. On their own. Are you going to throw that back in their faces?"

She let her head fall back against the chair and stared up at the ceiling. "I don't know."

"Jodie, you've always been such a fighter. This mystifies me."

"What if..." Jodie's voice faltered before she was able to articulate the fear that had been eating at her since Sam first showed up at her condo door, demanding that she give them all a chance. "What if they try, but they just can't find it in their hearts to let me back into their lives?"

"What if you fail?" her mother asked. "Would you be any worse off than you are now?"

"Part of me thinks I would."

JODIE HAD THOUGHT SLEEP would be impossible, but she passed out almost as soon as she got into bed. The instant she woke, though, depression washed over her. Her father was in the hospital; that was a definite downer. But more than that, she was being a coward about facing Sam and his boys, just as Sam had said, just as her mother had implied.

Jodie was deathly afraid of failing, afraid of losing affection. So she wasn't even going to try to rebuild something she might ultimately lose.

She was pathetic.

She and her mother drove to the hospital without saying much. Nadine was bright-eyed, hoping to see an improvement in her husband. Gentle Nadine Parker loved gruff Joe Barton and they had stuck together for years, even when Joe had hyperfocused on building his company and ignored his wife in the process.

Her mother put no conditions on love. If she had, she'd be long gone by now.

Jodie waited until Nadine had visited Joe and then gone to the cafeteria to get something to eat before she entered her father's room.

"It's good to see you looking better, Dad."

"I feel better than I did yesterday." He was hooked to an IV and various monitors, but his color was brighter and his expression alert. They made awkward small talk, then Jodie gave him the status report she'd gotten from Lucas over the phone a few minutes ago. Margarite had driven to the ranch early that morning and was there to answer the phone and hunt him down in the barn.

"Looks like Lucas is doing a better job than I'd expected. I guess he's earned that second chance."

Earned. Always earned. Jodie placed a hand on her father's arm. "Dad...do you believe in forgiveness?"

"I've never done much I felt I need forgiveness for."

"How about me? You were kind of...unforgiving with me sometimes."

"I just wanted you to achieve your fullest potential." He stared up at her, his gaze hawklike and unrepentant. "It worked, didn't it?"

Jodie simply gazed at him, amazed at the satisfaction in his weak voice.

"Do you want me to ask you for forgiveness for raising you the best way I knew how?"

Jodie shook her head. "No, Dad. But I need you to understand that pleasing you is no longer top on my agenda." Where it had been for as long as she could remember. She kept an eye on the heart monitor as she spoke, thankful the green line didn't blast to the top of the screen. She leaned down and kissed her father's forehead. "I hate it when you withdraw, but I can live with it." She shrugged philosophically. "I *have* to live with it."

Joe's eyes narrowed. "You're going to hook up with that vet, aren't you?"

"I don't know."

"You could do better," he muttered. Words she'd heard a couple million times over the years. Words she was going to have to get used to ignoring.

"That's debatable," Jodie replied calmly. Joe had approved of her first husband and that hadn't worked out at all. "Get some rest, Dad. I'll be back later." She was almost to the door when she stopped and said, "I love you, you know."

Joe didn't respond, but his heart rate increased an iota, just enough to let her know that her words hit home.

THE VET TRUCK WAS PARKED in front of the clinic and Sam was alone in the office when Jodie opened the door, the bells attached to the handle catching his attention. He stood when he saw it was her.

Jodie stayed close to the entry. "Why did the boys come to the ranch?" She spoke before he could, her voice remarkably cool and impassive—exactly the opposite of how she felt at that moment.

"Lucas needed help." Sam came out of his office and stood on the opposite side of the counter from her, tall, heart-stoppingly handsome, making her recall the day she'd gone nose to nose with him. "Beau needed to do penance."

"The letter?"

"The letter." Sam placed his hands flat on the Formica surface in front of him. "They're healing. Trying to move past what happened."

Jodie tilted her head, pressed her lips together. She wanted to believe what he said, but it was difficult when everything she wanted could evaporate in a heartbeat if the people involved came to their senses.

"Damn it, Jodie," he said, misreading her expression. "Look at what you're doing by not giving this a chance. I almost think *you* aren't interested in healing."

She felt her eyes widen. "Why would I heal?" she asked, perplexed.

Sam leaned across the counter. "You don't think you need to heal, too?"

She simply stared at him.

"We're all victims of Colin Craig, Jodie. Every one of us."

She pushed a hand through her hair. "I, uh, never thought of it that way." But it made sense. Enough sense that a lump was forming in her throat.

"You need to."

"I want to," she admitted in a low voice. Sam stayed where he was, with the counter between them, but his gaze never moved from her face. Jodie took a breath and asked, "Do you love me?"

"Would I have continued to chase after you if I didn't?" he asked in return. "I had many reasons not to."

"So that means you honestly believe we could build something. Even with...what happened to Dave and his wife?"

His expression was utterly sincere when he said, "I'm only interested in the future, Jodie." He came around the counter then, but stopped a few feet away from her, understanding her need for space. "I've learned a few lessons lately."

"Like what, Sam?" Her voice was barely more than a whisper, but he heard her.

"Like you can't control the things you want to control most. And there are no guarantees, no matter how much effort we put into not making mistakes. So…well, I can't say there'll be no losses, no mistakes, no heartaches. But I can promise to do the best I can, and to try to make what we have stronger every day."

Jodie didn't reply; she didn't know what to say.

Frustration flashed in Sam's eyes. "Damn it, Jodie, I can't change the past. But I can build a future."

"With me." She spoke flatly.

"With you." Sam matched her tone. "But it'll only work if we have faith in each other." He paused before he asked softly, "Can you do that? Have faith in us?"

His voice was steady, but the emotion she saw in his face was killing her. She started to speak, couldn't find the words, and then something inside her broke free.

She crossed the distance between them and reached up to take his face between her hands, loving the feel of his warm skin, the rough stubble of his beard on her palms. "How can I not have faith, when you refuse to give up?"

Sam let out a breath and pulled her against him, folding her in his arms and pressing his cheek against the top of her head. The phone rang.

"Damn it," he muttered, but he didn't move. If anything he held her closer.

"Why don't you answer that?" Jodie said after the fourth ring.

"Are you sure?"

She was tempted to say no, but she took the high road. This was part of Sam's life. "I'm sure." She tilted her head back so she could look up at him. "And whatever it is, I'll come along for the ride."

EPILOGUE

JODIE WALKED DOWN THE aisle on the arms of two men—her father and Beau Hyatt. Tyler stood next to his uncle as best man. Tears were streaming down her face before she reached the altar, and it looked as if Sam was going to join her. Her father kissed one damp cheek, Beau the other, and then she took her place by Sam's side, facing the pastor.

They weren't supposed to be getting married now. It wasn't in the plan they'd hammered out. Jodie still worked for the law firm in Las Vegas and Sam was overworked in Wesley, and they had agreed not to make anything official until the boys were in college.

Beau and Tyler had other ideas. They'd sat Jodie and Sam down one night, six months into their relationship, and explained that as entertaining as it had been at first, they were getting tired of the excuses and fake emergencies Sam and Jodie used when they wanted to spend the night together, and why didn't Jodie just move in with them?

Sam and Jodie had explained why that wasn't possible, but the kicker was, Joe had called Jodie and told her gruffly that if she wanted to marry Sam, then get it over with. That way maybe he could get free vet care. It wasn't until later that they discovered that Sam's nephews had waged a persistent campaign with Joe, too, which they'd eventually won.

So, on the first of October, Sam and Jodie were married in the city park, surrounded by friends and family and almost the entire community—many of whom still owed Sam money. Jodie knew he didn't care. Neither did she.

Later that night she had to drive back to Las Vegas, but Sam was coming with her, and in less than a month she'd be starting her own small practice in Wesley, using the money from her condo sale to buy the office building she would work out of.

Jodie didn't hear all the words the pastor said, but as she gazed up into Sam's eyes, she felt them in her heart.

She said, "I do," and so did he. Then they simply held hands and stared at one another until Beau called, "Hey, you gonna kiss the bride *or what?*"

Sam fought a smile as he kissed his new wife. "Or what," he whispered.

Jodie smiled before she kissed him back. "No arguments from me," she said. "Not one."

* * * * *

COMING NEXT MONTH

Available August 10, 2010

#1650 THROUGH THE SHERIFF'S EYES
The Russell Twins
Janice Kay Johnson

#1651 THE TEMPTATION OF SAVANNAH O'NEILL
The Notorious O'Neills
Molly O'Keefe

#1652 A LITTLE CONSEQUENCE
The Texas Firefighters
Amy Knupp

#1653 THIS COWBOY'S SON
Home on the Ranch
Mary Sullivan

#1654 RANCH AT RIVER'S END
You, Me & the Kids
Brenda Mott

#1655 A CHILD CHANGES EVERYTHING
Suddenly a Parent
Stella MacLean

HSRCNM0710

Spotlight on

Heart & Home

Heartwarming romances
where love can happen
right when you least expect it.

See the next page to enjoy a sneak peek from Harlequin® American Romance®, a Heart and Home series.

Five hunky Texas single fathers—five stories from Cathy Gillen Thacker's LONE STAR DADS *miniseries. Here's an excerpt from the latest, THE MOMMY PROPOSAL from Harlequin American Romance.*

"I hear you work miracles," Nate Hutchinson drawled. Brooke Mitchell had just stepped into his lavishly appointed office in downtown Fort Worth, Texas.

"Sometimes, I do." Brooke smiled and took the sexy financier's hand in hers, shook it briefly.

"Good." Nate looked her straight in the eye. "Because I'm in need of a home makeover—fast. The son of an old friend is coming to live with me."

She was still tingling from the feel of his warm palm. "Temporarily or permanently?"

"If all goes according to plan, I'll adopt Landry by summer's end."

Brooke had heard the founder of Nate Hutchinson Financial Services was eligible, wealthy and generous to a fault. She hadn't known he was in the market for a family, but she supposed she shouldn't be surprised. But Brooke had figured a man as successful and handsome as Nate would want one the old-fashioned way. *Not that this was any of her business...*

"So what's the child like?" she asked crisply, trying not to think how the marine-blue of Nate's dress shirt deepened the hue of his eyes.

"I don't know." Nate took a seat behind his massive antique mahogany desk. He relaxed against the smooth leather of the chair. "I've never met him."

"Yet you've invited this kid to live with you permanently?"

"It's complicated. But I'm sure it's going to be fine."

Obviously Nate Hutchinson knew as little about teenage

HAREXP0810

boys as he did about decorating. But that wasn't her problem. Finding a way to do the assignment without getting the least bit emotionally involved was.

Find out how a young boy brings Nate and Brooke together in THE MOMMY PROPOSAL, coming August 2010 from Harlequin American Romance.

HAREXP0810